Family in the Attic

Family in the Attic

A Novel

Elizabeth R. Pettiford

This book is dedicated to and written with heartfelt gratitude for my teachers who inspired it: the elderly, their families, and the medical community with whom I've worked.

I'd especially like to thank the residents of the small assisted care facility for the elderly I owned and managed. These residents most clearly demonstrated to me the enormous and oftentimes overlooked healing power of love and connection to community that is so essential when it comes to tending to the deepest needs of a bruised and tattered heart in crisis.

I would also like to thank my husband, Ron, who has always strongly encouraged my exploration of the road less traveled.

Contents

Chapter One

Sweet &
Sour Memories

CLARA'S SLEEP-FILLED EYES opened to a strange banging sound. Her eyes blinked, then searched every corner of her dusky living room. She didn't bother to move from her comfortable position, but wondered where the sound came from that woke her.

She allowed her old bones to relax a bit as she sat in her favorite blue and yellow plaid chair, its overstuffed softness hugging the contours of her small frame. Tan wool pants and a dark-brown sweater protected her from the winter's chill. Her outstretched legs were crossed at the ankle, and soft rose-colored slippers fit her feet snugly. She wore her wavy, salt-and-pepper hair short and pulled stylishly away from her face. Even in her aging years she held some of the beauty of her youth.

Clara continued to search the room for some indication of where the sound came from. Her eyes roamed the living room, scanning the family pictures on the fireplace mantle, and then the mahogany bookcase full of old family albums. At first glance, nothing looked out of place. She was perplexed. It upset her, and in some ways it frightened her that she couldn't get to the bottom of it. She'd heard the same banging sounds before, but had never been afraid before. Now she felt a little uneasy about living alone. Just as tension had begun to ooze from her body her eyes began to feel heavy, then she jerked violently, with a stabbing pain in her chest. She held her breath for a few moments while her chest pounded. Rolling her hands tightly into a ball, she squeezed her eyes shut to prepare for whatever was happening. Was this the end? Was she dying? Her chest heaved and she struggled to regain control of her breathing. She unclenched her hands, readjusted her position, and inhaled. Then she puckered her lips, allowing air and tension to flow slowly from her body, as if she were blowing out a candle.

Several minutes later she scanned her body for pain and sighed with relief. Her breathing slowed as the discomfort in her chest abated. The thought of having a heart attack alone in the house with no one to call out to for help was too frightening to ponder. She was still trying to get used to living alone. She missed the sound of a voice other than her own.

The last thing she wanted was to worry the children over nothing. She knew Robert and Darcy had busy lives, and worried enough about her as it was. She didn't want to add to their problems. She decided to just sit for a while and relax, and maybe have a cup of tea.

Or better still, a good stiff brandy! She smiled, placing both hands on her chest, and allowed her head to rest comfortably on the back of her chair as the tension continued to drain from her body. After a while, she slowly opened her eyes. All discomfort was gone.

The house was quiet except for the ticking of the grandfather clock. She stood up slowly. Her age was telling on her; the muscles in her body felt stiff.

It was still dusk and she knew she had no reason to rush. There was no place to go and no one to do anything for.

She walked over to the living room window. She could see the streetlights had come on; darkness had begun to creep its way into the house. It seemed a storm came out of nowhere. The wind began to bend the enormous oak tree across the street, causing its heavy, ice-ridden branches to bow their head as the wind passed through. She made certain there was no dizziness before setting out to turn on the lights. Each step was taken consciously and slowly as she continued to scan her body for discomfort, but none was found.

Deciding the wind must have caused the banging sound that woke her, she put it out of her mind. She couldn't remember if she had eaten lunch and thought maybe that's why she had a spell. She knew she should eat something, but didn't really feel hungry. On second thought, she knew putting something in her stomach was probably a good idea. She promised Robert she would eat, but it was no fun eating alone.

Instead of having a brandy, she decided on tea to go with a peanut butter and jelly sandwich. Afternoon and evening tea had been a ritual of hers for as long as she could remember.

She reached into her kitchen cupboard. The cupboard shelf held a collection of mugs of different colors and sizes. She always enjoyed selecting mugs to match her mood. It was difficult to decide which one she wanted. *Hmm, I think I'll use the flowered mug.* She smiled to herself, turning the mug around and around, reading the words "Happy Birthday, Sweetheart." She remembered Frank had given it to her. She sat quietly at the kitchen table sipping her tea and managing to finish half of her sandwich. She couldn't eat another bite.

Her mind was jumping from one thing to another, like a top spinning out of control. She was thinking about Darcy and Bret, her grandson. She hoped Bret had gotten over his cold and she wondered when Darcy was coming to visit. It dawned on her at that very moment that she still hadn't found her purse. She stood in the middle of the floor shaking her head as if that would clear it. *I'll need it later today to pay the paperboy. Let's see now—this is Friday, isn't it?* She scratched her head again. *No, what's wrong with me? It has to be Sunday. Robert was here for the weekend.* She didn't mind getting old, but didn't like the poor memory part of aging. She never wanted to forget the memories of her family she had stored away in her mind. They were all she had left.

She couldn't help wishing her time with her son hadn't been so short. Robert's busy life only allowed him a weekend now and then to visit his mother. Clara didn't complain; she was happy to have whatever time he could give. His wife, Jean, and his two children, Bret and Sara, needed him more. It amazed her that he was a grown man with a family. *Life certainly has a way of bouncing you from one situation into another,* she mused. One day a wife and mother, and the next a widow, and alone.

Clara found herself pondering how long she and Frank were married, and how many years had Frank been dead. She couldn't recall how long since Robert and Darcy had moved out on their own. The fact was, she wasn't sure anymore, and that bothered her too. She was annoyed at her failing memory about some things, yet, at other times, she could pull a memory out of her head as if it happened yesterday. *Aging should be graceful and kind,* she thought in protest. *Stiff muscles, failing memory, and chest pain aren't fair.* She could hardly bend over to put on her shoes—that is, if she could even find where she had put them. When Frank was alive and something went missing, the possibility existed that it might be his fault, but there was no one in the old homestead now except for her. Both Robert and Darcy were living their busy lives too far away for Clara to see them as often as she would like. Everything moved so fast, she felt like she couldn't keep up with all of life's changes. It made her wish she could turn back the hands of time.

Clara smiled, remembering a poem by Elizabeth Akers Allen, which she loved to recite now and then:

> Backward, turn backward,
> O Time, in your flight,
> Make me a child again
> just for tonight!

Just reciting the poem made her think of Frank, as she did so often. Since his death, Clara clung to the memory of him when he was kind, patient, and well. *Poor Frank,* Clara thought to herself. He loved his family, but he was a taciturn man who had difficulty showing emotions. In the beginning, when they were first married, he was fun and affectionate, but all that changed when he came home from the war. The children had never seen that side of Frank, the kind and fun side of him, the side of him Clara would never forget.

Frequently he would come home from work and greet her with a kiss, then from behind his back he would surprise her with a bouquet of roses. At first Clara would protest. "You shouldn't spend your hard-earned money on me," she'd say. He would take her in his arms and lovingly kiss her. "You're worth more to me than all the flowers on earth," he'd told her once.

Clara knew she had to find new ways to bring happiness into her life. She knew it wasn't going to be easy, but she was strong—and stubborn enough she thought—to slide gracefully into the final phase of her life. She looked down at her pale, wrinkled hands, then brought them to her face, gently following its contours, then stopped.

Sucking in air though her nose and exhaling, she tried to keep from crying, but she couldn't fight back the tears that found their way down her cheeks and dribbled into her mouth. Reaching into her pocket, she found a Kleenex, wiped her eyes, then blew her nose. *Control, old girl, control.*

She took the remainder of tea into the living room where she could put her feet up and rested. The events of the day had exhausted her.

Being self-sufficient was important to her now that Frank was gone. It was true that Frank handled almost everything from the day they were married. He felt strongly that a woman's place was in the home taking care of the children, cooking, and cleaning the house. He was the man of the family and it was his job to take care of all the financial needs. Clara never saw the checkbook or any of the bank statements. Frank paid the bills and took care of all money matters. If Clara needed money for food or for the children, she had to ask Frank for it. Since Frank's death, Robert stepped in and handled all financial affairs. She didn't argue with Robert about it. The fact was she was glad he wanted to do it; she wouldn't have known where to begin. Frank had done a decent job handling their money. Because of his astute business knowledge, she would be comfortable for the rest of her life. If everything went as planned once the house was sold, Robert and Darcy would have a hefty bundle. She wasn't by any means wealthy, yet she owned her own home, had a nice little bank account, and, thanks to Frank, she didn't owe anyone one red cent.

She inherited the family home from her parents, and it gave her great comfort to live there. She had grown accustomed to the familiar, still-lingering smell of tobacco from Frank's pipe and the creaking sounds of the wooden floorboards on the stairs. She looked forward to hearing the distant, distinctive whistle of the South Port cargo train in the pre-dawn hours and again at the end of a day. She enjoyed anticipating the sound of the church bells in the center of town that chimed on the hour. From her bedroom window she loved seeing Second Parish's big white church steeple in the distance, towering over the town and making the houses surrounding it look miniature in comparison. No question about it, Clara was a New Englander and couldn't conceive of living anywhere else.

She stretched her legs out on the footstool and looked around the room at all her familiar keepsakes she had collected over a lifetime. She focused on the pictures on the mantelpiece. There was a photograph of Robert and Darcy when they were small. Robert, the older of the two, was wearing a red bathing suit and sitting on the sand, proudly smiling at the camera. He had built a large sand castle; two of his fingers were raised in a victory sign while his other hand pointed at his creation. Darcy, sitting on the other side of the castle, smiled at the camera so that everyone could see she was missing three front teeth. Her dark-brown bangs were tousled by the sea air. The rest of her hair had been pulled and separated into two thin, short pigtails. Her green bathing suit outlined her tiny body. She held up both hands so everyone could also see that they were covered with mud.

Clara smiled now, thinking how much she had enjoyed watching the children grow up. Her eyes strayed to another picture, this one of Mary and her sitting on a park bench under a large elm tree. They were eating ice cream cones; the noonday sun shining through the trees had caused them to squint. In the picture, Mary towered over Clara even though they were seated. *How regal she looked then, with her long neck, her thick black hair, and her rich brown skin,* Clara mused.

The final black-and-white picture was of her wedding day. Her slender figure fit comfortably into a white velvet floor-length gown with long, lacy sleeves. An additional trim of soft lace traveled up to her neck, then circled down and across her breast. A single strand of pearls was her only adornment. She was beaming, looking like a storybook princess. Frank stood with great pride beside her, decked out in a black tux; his well-proportioned frame was a feature Clara found most attractive. His brown eyes and round face gave him the appearance of a young boy, younger than his actual years; his thin chestnut-brown hair was parted on one side. They had met in high school and married when he finished college.

The rest of the wedding party consisted of Frank's and Clara's parents in the front row with Clara and Frank; Mary, her bridesmaid; and David Thompson, Frank's best man, who stood in the back. Clara got up, and picked up the picture to take a better look at Dave. Gently, she put one hand to her lips and traced Dave's face. In the picture he was tall and handsome, with olive skin, thick eyebrows, and a moustache. He always wore his hair short. *It accented his kind face,* Clara thought to herself. A faint sense of sadness passed through her as she thought of Dave, like a breeze disturbing the leaves of a willow tree. *Time doesn't always heal.*

Glancing once more at the faces stretched across the mantle, she put back the wedding photo. She loved the people who had given her life purpose.

Returning to her chair, she put her feet up on the footstool again and relaxed her head on the back of her chair. Sighing, she closed her eyes; she felt tired.

Moments later, her eyes opened to the distinct sound of banging again. She looked around the room, and convinced herself it had to be her imagination.

Chapter Two

Lost in Reverie

CLARA RECALLED ROBERT'S BLACK Volkswagen speeding up the street as he left earlier in the day. She remembered feeling lonely, wondering when he would visit again. Standing in the doorway, she had wrapped her arms around her body to ward off the winter's chill. Heavy, dark clouds had covered the sun and were casting a shadow over the town. She and Robert had spent a wonderful weekend together, but he had to get back to his family as well as his medical practice in New York

Back inside the house she remembered to lock the door, and while she was at it, she pulled the shades down in the kitchen and the living room as she recalled her son's words of concern to her before leaving: "I'm worried about you, Mom. I hate it that you're living here by yourself. Other than Mary, you don't have another friend." He went on tell her not to forget to pull the shades, lock the door, and check the stove before going to bed at night. Clara had stood on her toes to reach up to hug him goodbye. As he bent down, she whispered in his ear, "You worry too much, dear. I've been taking care of myself for a long time." She said it all with a twinkle in her eye and jest in her voice.

Frank never made friends. He immersed himself into his work and discouraged Clara from making friends as well. She didn't want to upset him, so she kept to herself, except for Mary, her one good friend. Robert and Darcy felt she spent too much time alone, and it was true. She had backed away from Mary, her only friend, and was quickly becoming a recluse.

Whenever the children brought up the subject of alternative living situations, Clara turned a deaf ear; she insisted on staying in her own home. When the children came for visits, she wanted them to sleep in their old bedrooms. She purposely hadn't changed one thing since they left for college.

She loved her home and everything in it. She had hoped one of the children would keep the house in the family, though the prospect looked grim. Both had made lives for themselves elsewhere. It seemed small-town living didn't appeal to either one of them. She knew time could never stand still and all things had to change, but she was determined to not let anyone know how lonely she felt. She had to make everyone believe that all was well. The reality was that Clara *was* lonely. She missed her family. They were all that had ever mattered to her.

She decided to make herself a cocktail, her nightly ritual. It relaxed her and took the edge off her loneliness. She reached for the paper to read, then looked for her reading glasses. They had been in her purse, she thought, but she couldn't seem to find that either. It seemed to her she spent half her day looking for this and that. With a sigh, she decided to just sip her cocktail and head to bed. Her day had come to an end. She was happy to have spent it with her son.

The following day, she tried to do a little housework, hoping she would find her purse in the process under a pile of newspapers or at the bottom of the overflowing laundry basket. She stopped now and then when she felt tired. Pacing herself was important; she tired easily these days. She didn't mind doing chores, but found it difficult to do anything that required bending or pushing. She simply didn't have the strength for it anymore.

She stopped sweeping the kitchen floor and sat down at the kitchen table to catch her breath. She could remember when she was able to clean the entire house in a couple of hours. Now she was lucky if she could clean one room in an hour. Both Robert and Darcy had been nagging her to hire a housekeeper, but until now she couldn't imagine anyone other than herself cleaning her house. She decided to do what she could and not let it bother her. There was no one there to see it anyway.

If she let on to the children how she was really feeling, they would start talking again about her going to a nursing home, and that was something she couldn't think of doing. Wild horses couldn't drag her from her home. If her prayers were answered, she would take her last breath sitting in her favorite chair in the living room, or in her bed.

She was thankful Frank had been able to die in their home. It was the one thing he'd wanted, and she was glad his wish was granted. The thought of having to leave her home was just too painful to think about. Putting it completely out of her mind, she went about the day trying to busy herself.

She made herself a cup of tea. The mug she chose read, "The Golden Years." Suddenly out of nowhere, the image of Frank in his deepest depression came to her mind. She remembered how he would spend days in the bed; he had no appetite and would sit and stare into space as if he were trapped inside of himself. Clara tried to get him to talk about what was bothering him. She begged him to see Dr. Hoyt. The jolt of remembering Frank's dismal predicament made her see that she was heading down a similar path. Most of all she hated feeling isolated. She knew that she would have to pull herself out of the rut she was in. She couldn't change the past, but she certainly could turn the present and the future into whatever she wanted it to be.

She took her cup of tea into the living room and looked around at all the dust that was collecting on the furniture, along with piles of unread newspapers and dirty dishes. She sat and stared at the compounding disarray. She vowed to get busy. The housework she had started earlier in the day had hardly made a dent. No more spending hours in the children's rooms looking at the pictures. It was going to be difficult because there was one of Robert when he graduated from high school that she loved and another over his desk that housed twenty of his favorite baseball cards. Expensive collectors' items now, Robert had collected them free from packets of bubble gum.

At the same time, it would be hard not going into Darcy's room, which still had a floor-to-ceiling bookcase loaded with knickknacks and books she had collected over the years. She couldn't bring herself to throw anything away. Clara tried to recall where Darcy's dolls had gone. She didn't remember selling them or giving them away. She kept forgetting to ask Darcy what might have happened to them. She felt reasonably certain that she'd saved every one of them, but where she didn't know.

At times she would unfold and fold the clothes in their drawers. Other times she would simply sit in their rooms with her eyes closed, hoping to feel better just by being among their things. Everything was going to change. She was determined to stop moping around. She wanted to get busy. It was time to empty Robert's and Darcy's bedrooms of stuff neither one of them wanted. She took her empty cup of tea to the kitchen and began tidying up. She wiped down the counter; she washed, dried, and put away all the dishes that had accumulated in the sink over the past few days. She swept and washed the floor. Then with her remaining energy, she decided to cook herself a nice meal for a change. It felt good to her to be doing something.

The thought of Mary popped into her mind and she decided to invite her for dinner the following day. That would give her enough time to get everything ready. But when she opened the refrigerator, all she saw was half a loaf of bread sitting beside a jar of peanut butter, some jelly, four eggs, half a stick of butter, and milk—all the food that Robert had brought for her the last time he visited. She admitted to Robert that she had forgotten to grocery shop. Robert tried to leave enough food to keep her going for a bit, and Clara appreciated his help, but told him she was perfectly capable of doing her own grocery shopping in the future.

She knew she was getting a little forgetful. More than once she would search the house for her glasses, only to find them on top of her head. But forgetting to buy food, that was pretty bad. Her mind flapped to Mary; she liked the idea of inviting her for dinner. She would plan a nice, delicious meal. Wiping her hands on her apron, she called Mary. They chatted for a while. Mary told her how happy she was that she was getting out of the rut she'd been in.

She decided to do laundry since she was down to her last pair of underwear, and she got a big surprise when she lifted the top of the laundry basket to find her purse sitting there on top, her reading glasses tucked neatly inside. Smiling and relieved, she believed her discovery must be a good omen.

Chapter Three

Memory Lapses Worsen

THE FOLLOWING MORNING, WHEN Clara opened the front door, she could see the wind blowing the tree limbs, causing them to bend and twist. It blew her hair out of place and cold rain stung her face. She jumped when the closet door behind her slammed shut. It was quite a storm.

Closing the door, she was sure the banging sound she heard had to be a loose shutter banging up against the house. There was no sense worrying about it now. She knew she wasn't going out in that dreadful weather. She made a mental note to call Mary and reschedule their dinner for the next day to give her time to buy food. She thought she'd call her neighbor Bruce and ask him to check to see if a shutter had become loose from the storm. She knew it was a darn good thing she had a nice young man to give her a hand now and then.

Bruce Faraday was Darcy's age. He stayed on in the family house after his parents passed away several years ago. Now it was just him and his dog, Pepper, a cute little five-year-old mutt he picked up at the dog shelter. It was just like him to want to rescue a poor, helpless animal.

Clara liked Bruce. Who wouldn't? He was good looking, intelligent, polite, and most of all, he was crazy about Darcy. To Clara's regret, Darcy unfortunately regarded him as a friend and nothing more. She suspected he preferred living his life fancy-free. He certainly made a good neighbor; she knew she could count on him to do small repair jobs inside the house when it was necessary, and shovel when it snowed. Knowing he was there was comforting to her. Once, since Frank's passing, Clara tried raking leaves. Bruce spotted her and came running out of his house in his bare feet scolding her for not calling him to help her, while he gently took the rake from her, and she let him.

Later in the day Clara decided to make herself a sandwich for dinner, but was interrupted at the sound of the doorbell. She wondered who would be crazy enough to come out in this weather. "Mary!" she said with surprise at seeing her friend at her door. "What are you doing out in this terrible weather?"

"You invited me for dinner, don't you remember?" Mary stepped into the house, placing her shoes on the rug just inside the kitchen door in the hall, and followed Clara into the kitchen. She spotted the sandwich.

"So, are we splitting a sandwich for dinner? Or did you forget you invited me?"

Clara admitted she had planned to call Mary and reschedule dinner for another time, but she just forgot. She was embarrassed that she couldn't even throw something together since there was nothing in the refrigerator to toss together. Even the cupboards were bare.

"I've been trying to get you to come to my house for weeks. Would you like to have leftovers with me and we can have dinner at your house tomorrow?" Mary asked. Clara agreed.

Chapter Four

Frank's Depression Out of Control

CLARA FORGOT HOW GOOD it felt to get out of the house. She and Mary enjoyed the meal and the visit. She was tired when she got home and thought that when her head hit the pillow, she'd be fast asleep, but instead she lay awake reminiscing about Frank. She could never forget the night he died, finally released from his suffering from lung cancer. The children were both busy with their own lives. Diane, the hospice nurse, had arrived with pain medication. Diane knew Clara had put a cot in his bedroom so she could be near him. She was relieved when Clara told her Mary came every day to help. One day, after Diane had left for the day, the final moment came. Clara recalled that she had just finished the dishes and had gone into Frank's bedroom. She thought he was sleeping. She tried to read a book, but couldn't concentrate. She got up and went to him, when he murmured her name. She sat in the chair next to the bed and took his pale, limp hand in hers. He refused the pain medication she offered him. His hands were clammy.

"I have to tell you something," he murmured, his eyes closed and his breathing shallow. Each word was pronounced slowly and laboriously. Clara put her ear next to his cool lips so that she could hear his weak voice, which had become no more than a whisper.

"Clara," Frank continued after a pause. "I'm sorry I was hard to live with. I wish ... things could have been different between us. Try to enjoy life, Clara. You deserve it." His head fell to one side and he was gone.

Clara sat motionless, as tears ran down her cheeks. He was gone; his battle had ended. No more suffering and pain. He had put up a good fight. She wished things could've been different between them too.

Before his cancer, Frank had suffered from depression. It had altered his life. It had pulled the rug out from under him. The transformation in him had been difficult to accept. He was subject to mood swings, and they only grew worse. Clara feared he would never change, at least not for the better. She felt trepidation over how bad it might get. Regardless, she made the best of it. She did what a wife should do for her husband. She took marriage seriously. The words, "till death do us part," had meaning for her.

It wasn't easy living with Frank, but what choice did she have? He was the breadwinner. Clara had none of the skills required to obtain a lucrative job, one that could provide for the children. She had always admired her mother's courage; she had stood by her husband, Clara's father, through thick and thin. Clara decided she could do the same.

"You don't give up when things get tough. You get tougher," her mother's voice echoed down through the years. When the subject of Frank's depression came up, she would smile and say, "Pick your battles, Clara. That's what I always did with your father." Clara tried to be strong, as her mother suggested, but there were times when the only thing that got her through it was a cocktail. Frank didn't approve, so she became a closet drinker. She kept it from Frank until one day the cat got out of the bag. Looking back on it, Clara wished she'd stood up to Frank sooner.

She'd been cooking dinner and had decided to have a drink before Frank and the children came home. She usually allowed herself one drink in the evening. The top shelf in the back of her bedroom closet was her hiding place. Standing on a chair she reached up and fumbled for the bottle she thought she'd find. All she found in the closet shelf that day was a surprise: the bottle was gone.

She came down from the chair to find herself face to face with Frank, holding the bottle in his hand. "Is this what you're looking for, Clara?" he asked her.

They argued about her drinking. Frank insisted no wife of his was going to drink. Clara retorted that she only had a cocktail before dinner. What harm could it do? The argument went on all evening. Then came the silent treatment, which went on for days. Frank refused to discuss the subject any further.

Everything came to a head one afternoon when Frank came home from work and found Clara sitting at the kitchen table having a drink. He was livid.

"Clara," he yelled, "I forbid you to drink in this house."

Clara raised herself up from the chair and turned to face him. She spoke softly at first and then her voice began to get louder. "Frank," she replied. "I'm not a child, and you're not going to tell me what to do anymore. Either get over it or ..." The words wouldn't come out of her mouth. She thought about what Frank insisted. Then she lowered her voice. "Or I'm leaving you, Frank," she said quietly.

He stood looking at her, stunned. For the first time in their marriage, Clara stood her ground. He turned and walked out of the room. It took almost a month, but Frank gradually got over it.

Frank's mood swings got worse. Clara didn't want to upset him and she knew he couldn't help being depressed, so she tried to go along with whatever he wanted, keeping her mouth shut most of the time and picking her battles. She figured he would get over what was bothering him sooner or later.

He was a good man. He loved the children in his own way. He just didn't take the time to enjoy them. He was too busy with his furniture business. It was important to him to provide for his family. He couldn't see that he was missing the best years of their lives.

Clara couldn't help wondering how much Frank knew about her and Dave. One evening, Clara had come home and found Frank sitting on the couch with his head in his hands. He told Clara he had done something he wasn't proud of, and needed to get it off his chest. She sat next to him on the couch and put her hand on his. "What is it, Frank?" she had asked.

He looked as though he had been crying. He told her he had opened a letter that belonged to her. He told her he was looking for legal papers in the bedroom closet when he stumbled on a small trap door in the back of the closet.

He got on his hands and knees, he said, and squeezed into the tiny space and opened the door. Through the dark opening, he could see a gray metal box. He pulled it into the light and put it on the bed to investigate the contents. He wondered if maybe Clara had put the box there and forgotten to tell him.

It was a Saturday morning and he was alone in the house. Clara and the children had gone out for the day. The box contained a few newspaper clippings and cards Clara had kept over the years. He was about to close the lid when he noticed an envelope. Curiosity got the best of him. He picked the envelope up to get a better look. *It was addressed to me,* Clara thought to herself, remembering his words. The forwarding address was from Dave Thompson. Looking over his shoulder, he told her, he had made sure he was still alone in the house. He told her he had put aside his guilty feelings about opening up someone else's mail and sat down on the bed to read the letter.

Dear Clara,

It was harder than I expected for me to be at your wedding. I stood in the background during the ceremony trying hard not to cry. The pain I felt was a selfish one. I wished it was me standing next to you, not Frank. He's a lucky guy. I know it was a difficult decision for you to make. I just hope you will be able to live with it.

It's just like you to do what your parents wanted and not what you wanted. You can be sure I only want you to be happy. At least I have the memory in my heart that you will always love me, as I'll always love you.

I will not write again.

Love,
Dave

Frank told her he couldn't believe his best friend and his wife would hide something from him.

His pride got the better of him, and he did something that both shocked and relieved Clara at the same time. "You married me, Clara, not him. I'm glad Dave lives too far away to interfere in our lives. I'm going to try to let my resentment go, and I don't want to know what went on between you."

With that, he folded the letter up and put it back in the envelope. He kept the pain of what he didn't know about his wife and his best friend locked in his mind for more than forty years. Even though Frank never spoke of the letter again, it seemed to Clara that, from that day on, something was missing from their marriage.

Clara thought of another time when Frank's depression was out of control. Frank loved having a son; he cherished the day Robert was born. He spent hours playing with him. As soon as the boy could walk, he started grooming Robert for the furniture business. He took him to the store on Sunday afternoons and let him play with his toys in the office while he worked at his desk; Sunday was his day to catch up on paperwork. He wanted more than anything for his son to take over the business.

Once Robert was old enough, he began refusing to go to work with his father. Frank began manipulating him into going, promising to increase his allowance or letting him stay up later on Saturday nights.

Frank envisioned that his son—someday, maybe even a grandson—would run the business. He made it clear to Robert how important it was to him. Clara didn't like the way he pushed the business onto Robert. She always felt the children should do whatever they wanted, but she never said a word. Frank had made up his mind, and she knew trying to change it would be impossible.

The stubborn side of Frank was difficult to deal with. Once when Robert was in high school, she had tried to intervene, trying to convince him that he shouldn't push the issue so hard. They were sitting in the kitchen having coffee after the children had gone off to school. She put down her cup, cleared her throat, and sat straighter in her chair, as if to brace for an uncertain outcome.

"Frank," she began quietly, "Robert asked me to talk to you about the business and ..." Slowly Frank lowered the paper he was reading and placed it carefully on the table. His eyes were at half-mast, like the slits of the eyes of a wild animal before it attacks its prey. He glared at her icily.

Pronouncing each word slowly and deliberately in a quiet, deep voice, he said, "Clara, I'm going to say this to you just once. I never—do you understand me—never want that subject to come up again. My son is going to take over the furniture business, and you will support me in this. Do I make myself clear?"

"He—" Clara began, but Frank raised his voice in a thunderous roar.

"Clara," he yelled again, this time jumping up from the table and throwing his cup to the floor. She stared at the broken tiny white china pieces. Then he turned and stormed out the door.

Clara sat shaking in her seat, her heart pounding with fear. She couldn't believe what she had just seen and heard. She was thankful the children weren't at home to witness what had happened. She could take it, but the children couldn't. Frank was out of control and his behavior terrified her.

He was fun when they were first married. They enjoyed their life together. They looked forward to dining out and dancing. But after the war, the Frank Clara had married became someone else. The children saw less and less of him. He dove into the business and worked long hours—seven days a week. His depression worsened, and he slipped deeper into a world of his own.

He never spoke of it again, but Clara knew how much he had hoped Robert would take over the business. Robert had gone along with it until he finished high school, but once he started college, he discovered that his dream was to become a psychologist. Clara was proud of him and glad he was honest with himself and with his father about what he wanted to do. Frank didn't like it, but he never let on to Robert just how disappointed he was. But the fact was, his heart was broken.

Frank's depression worsened to the point where he couldn't sleep and had no appetite. Reluctantly, he went to Dr. Hoyt, who prescribed medication he hoped would help Frank cope. The doctor tried to get Frank to go into the hospital for treatment, but he refused. "What do I need a hospital for?" he'd asked. "I'm not crazy."

"That's right, Frank. You're not crazy," Dr. Hoyt had assured him. "But you *are* depressed, Frank, and we have treatments that can help. I admit there is no cure, but at least we can treat the symptoms."

"I know I get a little depressed once in a while," Frank had admitted, "but I can handle it. Look, Doc, I agreed to take the medicine, but that's as far as I go. End of subject." And it was.

It was late when Clara's mind stopped spinning from her memories of Frank and she was finally able to drift off into sleep.

Chapter Five

Father & Son Conflict

ROBERT WAS TALL AND handsome. When he smiled and showed off his perfect teeth, kindheartedness exuded from his face and he resembled his mother. He was constantly pushing his black-rimmed glasses back up his nose; it was a habit he wasn't aware of.

Robert studied psychology in college and made the decision to become a practicing psychologist, secretly hoping to help his father with depression—his way of giving back and making up to him for not wanting to take over the furniture business. His practice was successful and he loved what he was doing. In due course, he fell in love with Jean, a lovely young girl he had met in college. Soon they were happily married with two children.

Clara loved the fact that her son was a devoted husband and father; she couldn't be prouder of him.

Even with his busy life, he always found time for her. She looked forward to his visits, and his weekly phone calls meant a lot. After spending the weekend with Clara, he headed back home, leaving his mother alone again.

∞

Robert stopped at the intersection of Chestnut and Hawthorn Streets and waited for the light to change, adjusting his rearview mirror while he waited—and thought. He couldn't get the picture of his mother standing in the doorway and waving goodbye to him out of his mind. While he loved visiting her when he could, leaving her alone in the house without his dad was difficult, although life with Dad had certainly not been rosy for her. Still, at least she wasn't alone. Robert recalled the fights, the silences between them, and he also recalled the beatings he'd taken from his father. His dad actually believed he needed to make a man of his son. His mother kissed away his pain, and tried to stand up for him, but those memories were painful.

Now he had his medical practice, he understood the suffering that went along with depression. It always amazed him how his mom stayed with his father all those years of their marriage, jumping to his commands, afraid to upset him, which would have turned into an argument.

He never forgot the time when Darcy and he were kids stealing apples from the tree in Mary's backyard. He recalled his father never said a word to Darcy about it; he said she didn't know any better and that Robert should be setting examples for her since he was the eldest. He got spanked for it. His mom begged for his father to stop. "He's just five, Frank," she pleaded. "He doesn't know any better."

"He'll know better when I get finished with him, Clara!" he yelled. "Now don't interrupt when I am correcting the children."

Clara backed away that time, her head hung low. *I owe Mom so much,* Robert thought. *How can I ever repay her for all the years of her love for me and Darcy?*

Working at the furniture store was Frank's life and he loved it. But Robert knew it could never be his life. His dad tried his best to convince Robert to work there, and eventually take it over. There was a time Robert thought Frank hated him for that.

"You can make a good living at this for yourself. Don't be a fool, son. You can pass it on to your own son," Frank yelled one night when the argument rose again.

"Dad," Robert pleaded, "it's not what I want to do."

"If you're still thinking of psychology," he replied, "you're not going to make any kind of living at that. It's sissy stuff, anyway. If you think I'm going to spend money sending you to college for that crap, you're nuts."

"I'll get a job and pay for it myself, then," Robert answered. "I just don't want to work in a store all my life." Robert remembered how close he was to tears at that moment, and he remembered what he'd said in response. He made himself as clear as he could be on the subject: "I want to be a doctor, not a retailer."

That's when Frank got up from his seat and stood over him, his hands balled into fists. He glowered and Robert thought he was going to kill him. He got into position to defend himself.

Frank looked up and saw his wife standing in the doorway wringing a towel, fear written on her face. "Just get out of here. I'm done with this conversation," was all his dad said, once he knew he had a witness.

There were times when Frank's depression pulled him into the darkest pit of hell. He refused to be hospitalized; he felt there was a stigma attached to it, as so many people his age did in those days.

It wasn't until Robert was married with a family that he and his dad finally resolved their bitter relationship. And then his father was diagnosed with cancer.

In the last days, Robert went to visit him. He was under hospice care by then, and Robert was shocked by how weak he had grown. His skin was ashen, and he'd lost a lot of weight. He looked like a prisoner from a concentration camp. His brown eyes had lost their life force.

"Come in and sit down, son. I want to talk to you," Frank said. Robert was nervous.

He pulled up a chair and sat next to his dad, trying hard to fight back the tears that had welled up inside of him at seeing a once-strong, vibrant person reduced to skin and bones. He wouldn't let Frank see him cry.

Frank weakly took Robert's hand, lifted it up to his cool, pale lips, and kissed it. "Forgive me, son," he said feebly. "I have been a selfish old fool for trying to make you take over the business. Can you ever forgive me?"

Robert squeezed his hand. The tears fell in spite of his efforts to hold them back. "I've always loved you, Dad. I'm going to make you proud. I'll work hard ..."

"Stop, son," Frank said. "You don't have to do anything for me. Do it for yourself. That's good enough for me. I'm dying. You have your whole life to live. Live it to the fullest. Don't be a fool like me."

"You couldn't help it, Dad. You were sick."

"I should have done a lot of things differently, son. You're the man of the house now. Take care of

your mother. I made her suffer because of my selfish-
ness. I was jealous. She's a good soul. Darcy's a
fighter. She'll be fine. She'll have to find a man who
can handle her," he said with a half-smile.

*That's the way I want to remember Dad, with
that half smile,* Robert thought.

Chapter Six

Trip to the Police Station

C LARA GOT UP AT six, her usual time, put on her green velveteen bathrobe, and went downstairs to make coffee. While she was waiting for it to brew, she looked around at the dirty dishes from the night before and decided she would wash them. But first she needed a cup of coffee to clear her mind. She had forgotten to call Bruce about fixing the shutter, and decided she better write herself a note to call him before the day ended.

Suddenly, she jumped at a loud noise. It was the banging sound again. Glancing out the window, she could see the wind had stopped. The storm was over. The weatherman predicted sunshine. She opened up the back door to get a better look. The cool, crisp morning air was still. The sun was fighting its way through the clouds.

Next, she headed for the front door, speaking out loud as she went. "I wonder who would be knocking on the door at this time in the morning." No one was there. The morning air made her close the door and retreat to the warmth of her cozy kitchen. She sat at the kitchen table and waited for the sound to occur again. The house was still immersed in quiet. "Where are these annoying sounds coming from?"

Concerned, she bit her lower lip. She had a crazy thought and decided to give it a try. After all, there was no one to hear her. "Frank?" she called out tentatively. "Is that you making all these noises? You told me before you passed that you'd be looking out for me. It's nuts, but I have to ask: are you there, Frank?"

She looked around her kitchen, feeling silly to even think such a thing, but she had to admit she believed in ghosts, even though she herself had never seen one. "Frank, are you here trying to make contact with me, or frighten me out of my wits? If you're here, Frank, could you show me a sign?" Clara stood there intently, feeling crazy for talking to her dead husband.

She decided to get dressed and drive to the grocery store. The storm was over, and, although it was still chilly out, clouds gave way to sunshine, and she was sure the roads would be in good shape.

She frowned, thinking of how embarrassed and silly she was to invite Mary for dinner the day before and then not only forget to reschedule, but to not even have food in the house to offer her. She backed her old but faithful silver Chevrolet station wagon out of the driveway and was just about to pull out into the street when a horn beep startled her. Glancing out of her window, she was surprised to see another car too close to her for comfort. A young man rolled down his window and yelled, "Why don't you look where you're going!" Clara couldn't imagine what he was talking about. She was sure if he hadn't been speeding, she would've had plenty of time to pull out of her driveway.

"That's the trouble with young people today," she said to herself. "They drive way too fast."

She drove up the street, stopping at the stop sign, then turned left onto Main Street. She drove several miles and suddenly found herself on a highway. She had no idea where she was, and quickly pulled the car over to the side of the road. While the car idled in place, she sat with shaky hands on the steering wheel trying for the life of her to figure out where she was. Nothing looked familiar. Instead of the usual houses and the corner grocery store, she was looking at a four-lane highway. She swallowed the panic that was rising in her throat and decided that since she couldn't sit on the side of the road all day, she would have to drive to the nearest exit and ask for directions to the grocery store on Hancock Street. She felt ridiculous getting lost in her hometown. She drove for a while on the highway, apparently too slowly for the other drivers around her who honked and roared past her.

Eventually, she came to an exit. She thought she heard a siren blaring, but dismissed it as nothing and drove a few more minutes. Soon the unrelenting noise became so disturbing that she glanced up at her rearview mirror and was shocked to see a police car behind her with the blue light flashing. His arm was hanging out of his window signaling her to pull over. She pulled over to the side of the road as she was directed and came to an abrupt stop, pitching herself forward against the steering wheel. She couldn't imagine why she was being asked to pull over when she wasn't speeding, she was sure of that. A heavyset, older man with a protruding belly and a look of seriousness on his face approached her car and asked her to roll down her window.

"I've been following you for a couple of miles and you've been swaying over the yellow line, and didn't you notice that line of cars in the back of you?" he asked. "I'm stopping you, madam, for going too slow on a main interstate. I need to see your driver's license and registration please."

Clara fumbled for her purse and pulled her wallet out, but couldn't locate her driver's license.

"This is strange," Clara announced, embarrassed, "But it seems I've left my driver's license at home. You see, officer, I don't drive much these days and ..."

"Could I see your registration?" the officer asked, interrupting her.

"Why yes, of course." But when Clara couldn't locate her registration in her glove compartment, she knew she was in trouble.

"I'm going to give you a ticket for going too slow, reckless driving, and for driving without a driver's license and registration. Oh, and I'm also giving you a ticket for driving without a current safety sticker. The one on your windshield is two years old. In addition, I'm going to need for you to exit the vehicle please."

"Why would I want to do that?" Clara asked, annoyed. "I've got grocery shopping to do."

The officer raised one eyebrow and glared at her. "Because you are under arrest and I'm taking you into the station. You can arrange to have the vehicle towed."

Clara was both overjoyed and embarrassed when Mary came down to the station to get her out of jail. What started out to be a wonderful day ended in a total mess. With her driver's license revoked and no city buses, she was at the mercy of Mary to drive her wherever she needed to go. She knew Robert and Darcy would be disappointed, but not nearly as disappointed as she was in herself.

Mary took Clara to the grocery store and they spent a quiet evening eating a nice dinner that Clara had prepared at home. But all Clara could think about was losing her license and how she was going to live without being able to drive. The last thing she wanted was to be a burden to Mary. She sank deeper into a depression.

Chapter Seven

Bad Start, Good Ending

A S A CHILD, DARCY was different from Robert, who was sensitive and easy going. Darcy, strong-willed and stubborn, came out of the womb screaming and defiant, as if her role here on earth was to create animosity and discord within the family. She was an unhappy, tormented child.

For the first few years of her life, Darcy's screeching and tear-ridden face could be seen or heard by Mary who lived next door. She was sympathetic about how challenging it must be to live in the same house with a screaming child.

It seemed that nothing Clara or Frank did would calm Darcy. Clara tried holding and rocking her, she tried singing lullabies, she even tried letting the baby cry herself to sleep, but nothing helped. Dr. Hoyt kept assuring them that Darcy would eventually grow out of it. He checked her thoroughly and could find no medical reason for her screeching.

Darcy was still impossible to live with at eighteen months old. Because Frank had to get up for work, he resorted to sleeping on the couch. "Clara," he would shout at her in the wee hours of the night, "can't you do something to quiet that child? Call the doctor. There must be some medicine he can prescribe to keep her quiet."

Clara, more frustrated than Frank, retreated into her world of loneliness, and she prayed for a miracle. The sweet little girl Frank had hoped for was not what he got, and not willing to be patient during a difficult time, he retreated from her. It was Clara who gave Darcy love and understanding, though at times she secretly wished the child had never been born. She was horrified feeling that way about a poor, innocent child, but she was at a breaking point, and it pacified her cruel feelings. There was only so much a person could take.

Darcy was conceived in hopes that Clara and Frank's relationship would improve. Clara had come to think that his pulling away from her and not being intimate was her fault. She'd been convinced that having a second child would bring them closer. In fact, it pushed them even further apart.

As Darcy got older, her strong will just grew stronger. Clara often lost patience with her. By six, Darcy's temper tantrums were out of control. At her wit's end, Clara finally resorted to taking her for counseling. Frank didn't go for it at first, but then even he could see no other way. Their home was in a constant uproar. But after two or three visits, Darcy put up such a fuss about having to go that in desperation Clara finally took Mary's advice and stopped forcing her. Mary felt strongly that Darcy couldn't benefit from going if she hated it that much.

Clara welcomed Mary's advice. She was her best friend and confidante, and wise beyond her years. It was strange that even though Mary had never been married and had no children of her own, she had an innate understanding of children. Clara was sure her work as a nurse prepared her for helping to deal with Darcy's behavior. Mary, at times, could handle the children when they were being difficult better than either Clara or Frank. All Mary had to do was to give them one of her "I'm not playing with you" looks. Robert would freeze in place. Darcy would whimper until she realized she was not going to get her own way. If Mary couldn't handle Darcy, no one could.

After such a rocky start, Clara couldn't help feeling proud of how well Darcy had turned out. She grew into a beautiful young woman with a bright future in the insurance industry. She toiled her way up the corporate ladder, working hard to become one of the best and highest-paid executives in her field. Still, Clara couldn't help wishing that she would stop working so hard and traveling so much, and just settle down and get married. She wanted her to have children.

But Clara's relentless matrimonial urgings had not changed Darcy's mind in the least. Nothing had changed; she was stubborn and she had to have things her way. Dating wasn't important to her, and marriage was out of the question, or so she thought.

Clara had always wished something might have become of Darcy and Bruce's relationship. As far as Darcy was concerned, Bruce Faraday was a nice guy, the classic boy next door, but she had no interest in him romantically.

Their friendship began in high school. They had several classes together and spent a lot of time going to school activities. For a while Clara felt hopeful something might click for Darcy, that she would come to her senses and realize what a fine young man Bruce was. To Darcy, he was like an additional brother and nothing more.

Bruce, on the other hand, was crazy about Darcy from the day he first set eyes on her. At Clara's urging, Darcy had finally accepted Bruce's invitation to the senior prom. That was the night Bruce asked Darcy to go steady. It broke his heart when Darcy flatly refused him.

He began to distance himself from her after the rejection. It was more than he could take, watching her go out with other guys in their class. Then they both went off to different colleges and that put an end to the notion of anything ever becoming of it. That's when Clara had given up on the idea of playing matchmaker. Darcy and Bruce were simply friends.

Chapter Eight

Strange Banging Sounds Continue

IT WAS A DREARY, cloud-ridden afternoon. Clara wanted to read the book Darcy had sent her. Darcy knew her mother loved modern romance novels, but Clara couldn't get into it.

She couldn't concentrate. She began thinking of the children and what they might be doing at that very moment. Trying to change her train of thought, she thought maybe she would make some cookies, or she could call Mary to see what she was up to. Her mind was becoming cloudy and she felt like she couldn't think straight. Finally, she decided she didn't want to do anything. She placed the book on the table beside her chair and closed her eyes. Then she tried to think about her life without Frank and the children.

She was sure that Robert and Darcy were scheming up a way to try to get her to move somewhere close to one of them. Since Frank passed away several years ago they both were convinced that she shouldn't live so far away. She couldn't ever remember giving either one of them any reason to worry about her living alone. All this fuss about nothing was ridiculous. She only let the oil run out that one time, and she always locked the doors at night. And the driving business ... well, they didn't need to know about that.

It was true she hadn't been eating as well as she should since Frank passed away, but she didn't like cooking for herself, and she didn't have an appetite anyway. She felt there was no sense in eating when everything got stuck in her throat. Food was the last thing on her mind.

She just couldn't dream of leaving South Port. She'd lived there all her life. The very idea of Darcy trying to move her into a nursing home was just plain ridiculous. She wasn't going to leave her house, no matter what either one of them said. The house had been in the family for generations. She loved it, and wild horses would have to drag her out of it! Darcy would just have to let go of the idea. She decided that if she wanted to sit here and do nothing, then what business was it of theirs anyway? She would do what she wanted and that was that!

She relaxed her head on the back of her chair for what she thought was only a moment, but actually an hour had passed. She had no sense of time these days. One hour could seem like only a few moments. She uncrossed her ankles and sat up straight in her chair. She needed to stretch her back and shoulders.

She wondered if she had heard that familiar sound again. It was like someone or something was banging on the wall or ceiling. The wind wasn't blowing, so it couldn't be a shutter. The annoying sounds had been going on for the past few weeks or maybe longer; she wasn't sure. Oddly, it hadn't occurred when Robert was around. It slipped her mind to mention it because they were so busy enjoying each other.

Just then she heard something again, but it wasn't the banging sound. It was someone whispering her name. "Clara! Clara!" Closing her eyes, Clara covered her ears. *What in the world was that?* she wondered.

The noises were getting louder and more disturbing. Suddenly the voice stopped and the banging started.

It was time to start searching the house again. Clara went from room to room hunting for clues, listening for the strange banging sounds. *This is the strangest thing I have ever heard of. What is going on?*

When she was certain she was safe, she decided to give up the search. One thing she knew for certain was that it wasn't Frank. He was dead in his grave and he wouldn't be coming back.

Clara wanted to look at family pictures; it helped when she was missing family. She kept the thick, brown album on the coffee table where it was handy. She carried it out to the kitchen. She wondered where all the years had gone. Too often lately she would come across a picture of someone or someplace she couldn't remember.

She thought she should know who this person was or where a picture was taken. She knew she would figure it out, and if she couldn't, she'd ask Mary or one of the children, but it did bother her. She knew the not knowing was getting worse. The pile of pictures that she didn't recognize was getting bigger. She wished now she had written names on the back. She picked up a picture of Frank in his army uniform and smiled. He had a serious look on his face of someone who was proud; he was a patriotic man. Frank was fun then, before his depression. Her parents loved Frank. Clara didn't find out until after they were married that her dad had pushed them together. He didn't like it that Dave and she were becoming fond of each other. He wanted her to marry Frank because he was Catholic and came from a good Irish family. Clara found out once they were married that her father had insisted Frank come to dinner after church every Sunday.

There was one picture in particular Clara kept going back to, a scene that looked familiar, yet she couldn't recall where it was taken. It was a picture of one of the most beautiful sunsets that she had ever seen. Bright shades of yellow and layers of vibrant orange streaked the sky, offset by a magnificent blue-green sea. An occasional palm tree dotted the deserted beach. It was a place she tried to pull from the depths of her memory. She struggled, in vain, to recall the details.

Clara put down the photo and reached for a picture of Robert, sitting in his high chair smiling. His face and hands were covered with chocolate ice cream; it clung to his blue and white shirt. Minnie, the family bichon, was sitting at his feet, anticipating every drop that hit the floor. She was a small bundle of white fluff with big brown eyes and a cute little nose.

Next, she selected a picture of Darcy standing alone in the living room, dressed in a lavender floor-length gown. Robert, dressed in a white tee shirt and jeans, stood with his arm around her. His nose was wrinkled as he stuck out his tongue at the camera. Clara tried to recall when the picture was taken. She thought it must have been Darcy's senior prom.

Returning her thoughts to the present, Clara was sure that Darcy's nursing home idea came into her mind because it was what she wanted, but it wasn't what Clara wanted. Clara allowed Frank to control her for years. Now that he was gone, no one was going to dominate her again, ever!

Chapter Nine

Mother & Daughter's Concern for Each Other

JUST AS CLARA WAS slipping back into her reverie, the mysterious sounds came again. Her eyes searched the room. *There it is again!* She carefully made her way to the kitchen where she thought the sound was coming from. Over in the far corner near the back door, she heard it again. Bang! Bang! Bang!

She pulled aside the curtains at the back door to get a better look. The stray black cat Clara had named "Kitty" scampered off the porch. She couldn't remember when she had seen her last. Was it a few days ago, or was it a week ago? *It must have been her scratching at the door, looking for food. That's got to be the source of the noise,* she thought.

"Poor thing, you must be hungry out there in the cold," she said to Kitty.

Rummaging through the refrigerator, she found some leftover meatloaf from her meal with Mary and put it outside for her furry new friend. The bait was set; now all she had to do was wait.

After placing the food on the porch, she glanced at the wooden birdhouse hanging from the oak tree. Weathered with age, it had lost most of its dark-brown paint. Frank had built it long ago, she recalled; he had made several birdhouses over the years, situating them in various places around the backyard. Both she and Frank enjoyed watching the birds. Every season brought different birds for them to enjoy. Both of them agreed that the cardinal was their favorite.

From her bedroom window, she loved looking at the bright-yellow birdhouse Frank had made for her. For a moment Clara wondered if it was a woodpecker making those noises. Then she shook her head. No bird could possibly tap loud enough for her to hear it inside the house. Clara said aloud, "The old yellow birdhouse is still standing, Frank. It sure is nice to watch the birds during the day. I swear, I can sit and watch them by the hour. You know, the other day I saw two cardinals. Remember the summer they made a nest in the birdhouse?"

Clara's reminiscing was interrupted by the ringing of the phone. She was slightly annoyed at having to let go of a warm memory, but happy to hear the familiar voice on the other end.

"Hi, Mom. It's me."

"Darcy, dear, how are you?"

"I'm fine."

"I was just sitting in the kitchen looking at the family album. I love going through it. It's fun looking at you kids when you were young. You know, honey, there's a picture of an ocean scene with a beautiful sunset. I can't recall where it was taken. I wish I could remember."

"Maybe it's the place in Mexico where you and Dad went for your honeymoon," Darcy suggested.

"You know, I think you're right!" Clara laughed lightly. "How could I forget? How are you, Darcy?"

"Mom, I just told you I'm fine—but busy as usual."

Clara couldn't keep herself from asking the question that somehow managed to come up in almost every conversation she had with Darcy: "Have you met anyone special, dear?"

Darcy was quiet for a moment. She couldn't tell her mother about the man she was dating. She knew her mother never would approve of her dating a married man. "I squeeze dates in when I can," she replied instead, more than a bit defensively.

"That's good because life is short, you know," she said. "You should be having fun."

"I'm having fun, Mom. But I'm very busy too. I don't have a lot of time for dates."

Clara never bought the not-enough-time argument. "That doesn't mean you can't settle down with one man, honey."

"Are you eating right, Mother?" Darcy asked, abruptly changing the subject.

"Of course I'm eating right," Clara retorted. "I'm doing fine. Don't worry about me. I just want you and Robert to take care of yourselves and enjoy your lives."

"We wish *you* would enjoy *your* life more, Mom," Darcy said, continuing to press her mother on one of the subjects that she always brought up. Then she moved on to two others: "Have you started to pack up Dad's clothes for Goodwill yet? I hope you're not sitting around doing too much thinking about Dad. Have you thought of joining the senior center in South Port?"

"No, and I'm not going to either," Clara answered hotly. "That's for old people. I still have a little life left in me. I'm not as old as you may think, young lady."

"My other phone's ringing, Mom, I have to run. I'm at work—it's probably a call I've been waiting for. I'll call you later on or tomorrow. You call me if you need anything—you have my cell number so you can call me any time. Love you, Mom."

"Love you too, dear," Clara said quickly, but found she was speaking into a dead phone. Darcy had already hung up.

Clara sat, musing over the call. She wished Darcy would get serious about her life. She had more reasons for not getting involved with anyone. Then Clara began thinking about Darcy's main agenda for calling. She certainly couldn't let on that she knew she'd secretly been looking into nursing homes for her, and there was no way Clara could mention those annoying sounds she was hearing. That'd only fuel Darcy's suspicion of her being incapable of living alone. No sense starting an argument. One thing was for certain: she was never going to leave her home.

The day flew by and Clara's plans to clean her house or cook a wholesome meal were fading away. Each time she thought of something, she'd put it off to watch television. She tried reading, but couldn't concentrate. She kept thinking about Darcy. She just hoped and prayed she would settle down and find a nice young man, someone who would love and cherish her. Clara felt Darcy would stop fretting about her and would get on with her own life if she had a man in her life, a good man.

Chapter Ten

Mary to the Rescue

CLARA CHOSE A GREEN mug with the words, "Mother Knows Best." Darcy had given it to her. She sat at the table sipping her coffee and nibbling at her toast. The coffee tasted good to her, but the idea of eating had no appeal. She took a bite of toast and threw it down on the plate. It had no taste.

She was gazing out the window at the oak tree in the backyard where she had a good view of her favorite tree. She had seen it turn colors so many times over the years.

She became fully alert at the sound of someone knocking at the door. But when she got to the door, there was nobody there. She stood looking out onto the empty front steps, both hands on her hips, scratching her head in disbelief. Who would pull such a trick on her? She knew she had heard someone knock. She looked down and noticed the untouched meatloaf, right where she'd left it the night before. She had forgotten to check on it before she went to bed. It seemed Kitty wasn't hungry, but she left it out, knowing that she'd return when she was.

She sat back down and stuffed another bite of toast into her mouth. When the phone rang, she got up to answer it. It was Dr. Hoyt's office calling.

"Yes, this is Clara speaking," she said, still chewing.

"Oh, good," said Dr. Hoyt's cheerful nurse, Adele. "How are you today?"

"I'm just fine, dear, for an old lady."

"Dr. Hoyt just got the results of your blood work back. He wants you to stop taking the heart medication for one day, then take half the medication for three days, then take the medication every other day. Do you have any questions, Clara?"

"Would you repeat that again for me, honey? I don't hear as well as I used to. How many pills do I take?" Clara reached for a pad of paper and a pencil.

Adele repeated what Clara needed to do, then Clara hung up the phone with a sigh. Standing by the phone, she looked at what she had written down. It read, "Take the heart medication for three days then stop." *These young people talk so fast,* Clara thought to herself. *It's impossible to understand a word they say. I think I got it right.* Not giving it another thought, she put the slip of paper in her bathrobe pocket.

Hearing the knock again, Clara again went to the door. Again, there was nobody there. In her frustration, she realized she felt tired and short of breath. Grabbing her chest, she took a few deep breaths. Relaxation flowed through her body. *No need to have a heart attack getting up and down, old woman,* she told herself. She sat and relaxed for a few more minutes before placing her dirty dishes in the sink. The stack was mounting. She planned to clean the house later. She recalled her vow to get out of a rut and start doing things. She had become good at procrastinating. Suddenly she heard the knock again.

This time she went to the front door for a change, but again, no one was there. *What is going on around here? Am I losing my mind? Where haven't I looked?* She stood in the hallway thinking her way around the house. Then it came to her: the basement. It was as likely a place as any. Flipping on the light, Clara headed downstairs to the basement. Her eyes searched every corner of the room. It was pretty much empty except for a large black oil tank in the far corner, sitting on the cracked cement floor. A musty smell and chill hung in the air. She couldn't find a clue of anything that would cause a banging sound.

Climbing back upstairs was a chore. Clara hung onto the railing with both hands, and had to pause between each step. Once at the top, she sighed with relief. *I made it! I can't remember having this much trouble climbing the stairs before.*

Heading for the living room, she barely made it to her chair. Lowering herself into it, she let her head flop back against the cushion. She was breathing fast. She pressed both hands against her chest.

Panic gripped her, and she felt as if something heavy was sitting on her chest. She hoped she wasn't having a heart attack.

Fumbling for the phone on the table, she dialed Mary and told her what was happening to her.

"Stay put and try to relax," Mary answered tersely. "I'm on my way."

Mary quickly called 911 and gave them Clara's address. Then she hurried over to Clara's house, making it in record time.

Within minutes the ambulance arrived. Two emergency technicians found Clara slumped in her chair, her eyes closed, fighting back tears. Mary, who had been kneeling next to her holding onto her hand, moved aside. She fumbled nervously to remove the cool, moist cloth she had placed on Clara's forehead.

"We're here to help you," said a tall, older man with a shiny bald head. He knelt at Clara's feet and reached for his emergency kit. "Can you tell us what's happening?"

"I was having chest pain, but it's gone now. I asked my friend Mary to call you," Clara said weakly.

"Good thing you did," said the second EMT, a shorter, younger-looking man. "Just relax. We'll take good care of you." They directed as many questions as they could to Mary, who was standing close by, nibbling at her lower lip and wringing her hands.

The taller EMT took Clara's vitals and started oxygen, while the shorter one got ready to hook her up to an intravenous. While she was being attended to, Mary stepped back out of the way and glanced around the room, disturbed by all the clutter she saw. She couldn't believe it: she was doing such a good job keeping the place up, but she had slacked off and it showed. Clara always kept a neat house—this wasn't like her good friend at all, she thought. But she quickly put it out of her mind; Clara was sick and that was all she could think of.

While Clara was being attended to at the hospital, Mary stepped out into the waiting room to call Robert. Giving him a full report of what little she knew, she told him she had asked the doctor to contact him when they knew what the problem was. She promised him she would stay with Clara. He thanked her and said he would stay put at his office until the emergency room doctor called.

Mary hung up the phone and sat in the waiting room biting her lip, trying hard not to cry. *Poor thing,* she thought. *I pray she's going to be alright. I don't know what I would do without her. She's the closest thing to family I have.*

She put her head in her hands, covered her face, and prayed. There were several other people in the waiting room watching the television. She didn't want anyone to see the tears streaming down her cheeks. It wasn't like Mary, who always liked to stay positive. *Come on, Mary, get a hold of yourself. Clara's going to be fine. The last thing she needs is you sniveling over her. Poor thing is probably frightened to death.*

After several hours, a stern-looking young doctor of medium build approached Mary and escorted her to a small room. Both took a seat facing each other. Mary, picking nervously at her fingernails, held her breath for the verdict.

"Clara has given the hospital written permission for me to speak with you," the doctor started. "She told me you've contacted her son. I have as well. The family is welcome to call me if they have any questions. You can relax now. Your friend is going to be fine. I can see no reason why she can't go home."

Mary exhaled and wiped her eyes with a Kleenex the doctor handed her. It felt like a mountain had been lifted from her shoulders.

"I feel certain Mrs. Lewis has had an attack of indigestion. A second EKG should be done soon for comparison purposes. I've set up an appointment with Dr. Hoyt for tomorrow. You can take her home now. I'll have a nurse go over the discharge paperwork with you both."

On the way home from the hospital, Mary offered to stay with Clara just to make sure she would be okay.

"You've done enough," Clara said, gratefully. "You go home. Get some rest."

"I already promised Robert and Darcy I would stay with you."

"I wish you hadn't called Robert about this," Clara said, her lips tight with disapproval. "It was just a little indigestion. It was nothing serious enough to even keep me in the hospital."

"You can't keep things like this from the children, Clara. It could have been serious, you know. Clara, did you hear me?" When she didn't answer, Mary looked over at her friend. Clara was sound asleep, her head resting comfortably on the back of the car's front seat, her mouth wide open.

When they got home, Clara refused Mary's suggestion to go upstairs to nap. She said she didn't feel tired enough to sleep at the moment. However, within minutes she was sound asleep in her chair with her feet elevated on a stool.

Even the ringing of the telephone didn't disturb her rest. Mary picked it up on the first ring and spoke quietly to Robert, telling him Clara was asleep.

Robert was disappointed that they hadn't kept his mother in the hospital. He'd hoped they would have monitored her at least overnight. He asked Mary if she thought he should come home right away.

Mary suggested that he should call his mother in the morning and talk to her himself. She was sure Robert would know what to do once he spoke to Clara. Robert thanked Mary for staying with his mother. It gave him comfort knowing she was going to spend the night with her. Mary was glad to help. She told Robert that she was sure Clara hadn't been eating and that the house was a mess. Robert wasn't surprised at the news. He was worried about her and he wasn't sure what to do about it.

Later on, that evening, Clara admitted to Mary that she was happy to have someone in the house. Mary knew it had to be lonely living there by herself. It probably played a role in how poorly she was eating. In fact, she'd told Robert more than once Clara hadn't been eating right. Mary brought her homemade dishes now and then, but Clara barely touched them.

She appeared to be losing weight, and her house was unkempt, to put it nicely. Whenever the subject came up about not eating right, she just blew Mary off. She insisted that she took her medications every day, but Mary had her doubts. Clara flatly refused to see Doctor Hoyt. Whenever Mary made a comment about dirty dishes in the sink or not being able to see the coffee table or the couch anymore from all the newspapers covering it, she just said she'd get to it or she'd been meaning to clean, but just didn't feel like it. Mary offered to clean the house for her, but Clara adamantly refused any help.

Mary was sure Clara didn't understand how important it was to eat well. Clara had tons of cookies and candy around, which Mary was sure she filled up on. Robert knew everything Mary had been telling him was true. He also knew how stubborn his mother was. He so wanted her to agree to live with him, but he knew that was wishful thinking. Wild elephants couldn't drag her from her home.

Mary was sympathetic. She knew all this must be hard on Robert—it certainly was on her. Clara was her best friend. She only wanted to help. It plagued her to see her dearest friend like this. It seemed to Mary, Robert and Darcy that this change in Clara's behavior had been gradually getting worse.

Chapter Eleven

If Life is Just a Bowl of Cherries, Why Am I in the Pits

CLARA FORCED HER EYES open. Yawning, she turned on her side and focused on the oak tree through her bedroom window, the same oak she loved looking at from her kitchen. The sound of mourning doves made her smile.

She watched a male cardinal come to rest on a branch, looking for food with his keen eyes. Leafless limbs easily supported the weight of his delicate, bright-red body. He chirped as he hopped from branch to branch, letting the morning sun warm his wings.

Then the cardinal did something she had never seen one do before: he lingered on the branch he was on and boldly stared at her with his bright, keen black eyes. It was as if this cardinal wanted to make sure she would remember him. She couldn't take her eyes off the bird. It was the largest, most scarlet-red cardinal she had ever seen. Finally, he chirped several times and flew off.

Clara felt enveloped and embraced by an all-encompassing warmth, love, and sense of being protected that went far beyond anything she had ever experienced in her life. For an instant she swore she saw Frank's smiling face, or was it simply her imagination playing tricks on her?

Sundays were the one day of the week she allowed herself the luxury of relaxing in bed. Her eyes drifted around the bedroom at her favorite treasures. She stopped to focus on her grandmother's antique oak bureau and matching mirror. On top there were perfumes and powders she enjoyed using almost every day. These were gifts she had known she could count on from the children and Frank over the years. There was also a small black wooden box with hand-painted gold and red flowers that Frank had given her. Each of its three drawers had delicate glass knobs. He had made it for her the first year they were married. She smiled, recalling how clever he'd been with his hands.

She stared at a fine miniature doll sitting on the bureau given to her by her mother, its delicate facial features hand-painted onto its cream-colored porcelain face.

She let her eyes drift to the lace-curtained window where she'd just seen the cardinal. In front of it was an antique high-backed chair. The flower-embroidered red, white, and blue seat that covered it reminded her of her patriotism; it had been masterfully crocheted by her mother. Though faded, it was still in good condition.

It was impossible to choose any one favorite item in her home; she loved them all. They gave her life its richness. Clara closed her eyes and gave thanks for all of her blessings. It was a morning ritual.

Suddenly, she thought she heard the knock again. This time she was sure it wasn't Kitty. She pushed the covers off, and came slowly to a sitting position. She yawned and stretched her arms over her head. Wiggling her toes into soft rose slippers, she reached for her bathrobe, which was lying on the chair. Making a conscious decision to ignore the sound for a change, she lazily went downstairs to make coffee.

Once downstairs, she put the coffee on and sat gazing out the kitchen window while it brewed. The sky was gray and clouds threatened to bring more snow.

Mary's car wasn't parked in the usual place. She wondered if she had parked it elsewhere. She hadn't heard from her for a few days. She thought she would call her later on and see what she was up to. She felt bad because she knew she should see more of her.

Clara stepped onto the porch to get a better look, almost tripping over the empty plastic bowl of food she'd set out for Kitty. *What in the world is this bowl doing outside?* Picking it up, she held it in the palm of her hand trying to recall why it would be sitting on her porch. She knew she must have put it there. Where else would it have come from? Perplexed, she stood in the open doorway for a moment, scratching her head. Then she remembered she put it out for Kitty. She was glad to see she finally had eaten what she had left. But at the same time, she was sure now that Kitty was making the banging noises.

Still standing by the open door, she could see Mary's car was parked in her driveway instead of her own. *Now that's strange,* she thought. *Why would Mary park her car in my driveway?*

Closing the door, she returned to the coffee pot and poured herself a cup. She used a green mug with the message, "If Life Is Just a Bowl of Cherries, Why Am I in the Pits?"

She heard the banging sound, and it certainly did sound like it was coming from the back door. She jumped from her chair and headed for the door and opened it quickly, hoping to catch Kitty making the noise, but to her dismay, there was no sign of the animal. *Where in tarnation is that banging coming from? I'm getting sick and tired of this!* Frustrated, she returned to the table and her mug of coffee.

Placing her elbows on the table and putting her fingers together as if she was in prayer, she rested her chin on her fingertips to ponder the precarious situation. Suddenly she raised a fist in the air, tightened her lips into a straight line, and let her fist crash down onto the table, causing her mug of coffee to jump. *Nothing is going to drive me crazy in my own house. I am going to get to the bottom of this nonsense, if it is the last thing I do!*

She decided to search the attic. It was the last place to look. On her way upstairs, she passed the guest bedroom and wondered why the door was closed. Standing motionless outside the door, she held her breath. Someone was inside the room! Her heart was racing.

Placing her shaking hand on the doorknob, she slowly turned it and opened the door—and found Mary, dressed for the day, combing her hair in front of the mirror.

Mary was lost in thought. Before going to bed the night before, she had found a note in the pocket of the bathrobe that Clara had lent her. It mentioned changes in her medication from Dr. Hoyt's office.

The note was in Clara's handwriting, and she couldn't help wondering if Clara was taking her medication correctly. The words were misspelled and the directions simply didn't make sense. Why would the doctor want her to stop taking her medication?

"Mary, what are you doing here?" Clara asked. Mary looked up at her in surprise.

"I spent the night here with you, Clara. Don't you remember?" Clara had a blank look on her face and Mary's smile turned to a look of surprise. It was clear that Clara had totally forgotten. "Clara, an ambulance took you to the hospital yesterday for chest pain. Do you remember that?"

Clara didn't. "I remember calling you when I had chest pains," she said slowly. "The rest is a blank. Do you think I'm losing it?"

"You're confused, but that's probably from the medication they gave you in the hospital."

"I don't remember them giving me any medication," Clara said vaguely.

"Clara, I found this note in your robe pocket last night. Is this from Dr. Hoyt? Did his office call?" She handed Clara the slip of paper. "Have you stopped taking your medication?"

Clara stood shaking her head. She had no idea where the paper had come from. Furthermore, she had no idea what medication Mary was talking about.

The room was quiet. Neither one knew what to say. Clara was confused and embarrassed. Mary decided it was time to change the subject; she could see that Clara was close to tears, but she knew the confusion was something Robert and Darcy needed to know about as soon as possible. She was shocked at what had just happened. She would ask Robert to call Dr. Hoyt about his mother's medications. She had a sick feeling in the pit of her stomach that Clara had stopped taking them altogether.

Mary smelled the rich aroma of coffee and needed a cup to help clear her head. She picked a mug to go along with her mood; it read, "Friendship." She couldn't let Clara know how disturbed she felt about her declining memory; on the other hand, she was glad she was able to help her.

Mary let Clara chatter on about the children, but only half-listened. She couldn't get over Clara forgetting she had spent the night. She didn't remember a thing that had happened to her the day before. *She's acting like she has amnesia,* Mary thought. She was worried about her, but didn't want to show it for fear that bringing the subject up again would cause her to be in tears.

On the way home, all Mary could think about was how she was going to break the news to Robert and Darcy; she knew they would be even more worried than she was. It was one thing to forget to bring in the mail or the newspaper. But to forget going to the hospital, and possibly not taking her pills, that was a different story. Clara was getting worse.

Mary knew she would have to start checking in on her more. Clara needed help. Something was wrong and Mary knew it. She decided to make up a few more healthy meals for Clara to put in the refrigerator. She knew she wasn't eating well; peanut butter and jelly sandwiches was not healthy eating. In addition, she was losing weight. She had to admit she wished Clara would agree to stay with her son at least for a while, until she got used to living alone. Mary knew that some people just aren't able to live alone. Ultimately, Mary agreed with Robert. Clara was stubborn and nothing was going to drag her friend from her home, but something had to be done.

Chapter Twelve

Family of Imaginary Friends

ONCE MARY LEFT, CLARA headed for the attic. She was going to get to the bottom of the noise once and for all. She was sick and tired of being disturbed by banging sounds; who'd ever believe such a strange story?

The last thing she needed was for Robert and Darcy to think she was losing her mind. Robert was already concerned about her living alone, and Darcy was fully prepared to shove her into a nursing home. Hopefully Mary didn't think she was losing her mind. She had to find out what was causing all the noise or she knew she would go crazy. Time was running out.

Flipping on the attic light, she stood in the doorway looking around for any clue that might explain the strange banging sounds. A single lightbulb hung in the center of the room. She squinted, wishing the light was better. The entire ceiling was covered with cobwebs, as were the thick, dark beams that supported the roof. Floor-to-ceiling boxes neatly lined the walls on three sides.

In the far corner of the room, a weather-beaten window sat slightly ajar. Dilapidated floorboards creaked as she made her way over to close it. On the way, she spotted an old trunk tucked under a ledge, its shabby frame weathered by use. She struggled to pull it over to a nearby window to get a better look.

The anticipation of what was in the trunk mounted. When the top came up, there were all Darcy's old doll clothes. Clara pulled them out and inspected the beautiful handmade garments, some of which she had made herself. To her surprise, at the bottom of the trunk was a beautiful doll.

Clara turned the doll's face toward her and held her high in the air. Her frozen black eyes, turned-up smile, and blond curls made her look almost real. Her pink and white dress was torn and in need of a washing, as was the doll herself. "I think you'd look pretty if you had a nice bath and clean clothes to wear," she told the doll. "I could even mend your dress; goodness knows I've sewn enough clothes in my day. What do you think of that?" She wrapped the doll in a blanket along with all the doll clothes, and decided to wash everything.

A light from the window illuminated another area of more boxes on the opposite side of the room. Floorboards creaked again as Clara picked her way towards another trunk. Cold air from the window chilled her as she approached it; she pulled her green sweater around her to help ward off the cold.

As she approached the trunk, she tilted her head to one side, trying to recall how a trunk that size could have ever gotten in the attic. A handsome, handmade piece, its lid was trimmed with dark-brown leather. Although it was torn in places, it still retained its elegance. Large silver buttons were used in place of nails.

Approaching the trunk, she disturbed dust when she lifted the lid. She couldn't believe her eyes! It was filled with toys and dolls of all shapes and sizes. Taking hold of the handle, and with some effort, she dragged the trunk over towards the window to get a better look.

Overwhelmed with excitement, she pulled out another beautiful doll whose face, arms, and legs were made of porcelain. This doll had matted black ringlets surrounding her dark-brown face.

She picked up a third doll with big black eyes and long lashes. It had a small, turned-up nose, and cherry-colored lips that were painted in an everlasting smile. The doll's dress was as dirty as the other ones, but it was plain to see that it had once been lovely. Both of these dolls had lost their shoes and socks. Clara held them up to the light from the window and inspected every inch of them. She turned them around and upside down, admiring the way the dolls' clothes were made. Closing the lid of the trunk, she cradled them in her arms as if they were real babies.

Turning off the light in the attic, she carried the dolls downstairs to the kitchen, handling them as if they were three precious jewels, and felt happier than she had been in ages. She had no intention of telling anyone about the dolls, except Mary. She knew Mary would keep her secret. She would surprise Darcy and Robert when they came to visit.

Her first order of business was giving them a bath. "Don't worry, my little darlings, I won't get soap in your eyes," she told them as she rinsed them off in the bathtub. "I still remember how to give a baby a bath. Now, doesn't that water feel nice?"

Once the dolls were bathed and dressed, she would make them new clothes. "You can't wear the same clothes every day. I guess I have my work cut out for me, don't I?" She was having so much fun that she almost forgot about breakfast. She sat each doll at the table with her. "Now isn't this nice? We're having breakfast together!"

It felt good not to eat alone. For the first time in a long time, she cleaned her plate. She had made herself a decent meal for a change and she felt better than she had since Frank's passing. The dolls were giving her a new lease on life.

The kitchen was full of morning sun. The chimes of the grandfather clock resonated throughout the house. She looked out the window as she ate a slice of toast with strawberry jam. Her coffee mug read, "When I Am an Old Woman, I Shall Wear Purple."

Chatting away happily with her new companions, Clara giggled as she looked from one to the other. "Did I thank the three of you for making so much noise in the attic that finally I found you?" she asked them aloud. Clara was enjoying having something to do. She could never forget how to take care of babies. She had plenty of practice caring for and raising her own two.

The white and yellow curtains at the window over the kitchen sink were pulled to the sides to reveal a big oak tree in the backyard that almost blocked her view of Mary's house. A thin layer of snow covered the ground in the backyard. Sitting in the kitchen and looking out the window was a favorite pastime of hers, but Clara had other work to do. She really didn't have time to sit and look out the window; her new dolls needed her. She had a family to take care of!

After breakfast she tidied the kitchen. Now that the dolls were bathed, she began washing their clothes; she knew they would dry nicely on her clothesline. She could hardly wait to put their clean clothes back on them.

∞

Later that morning, Clara sat in her chair smiling as she looked over at the dolls, which were lined up on the couch like well-mannered children. A knock at the door made her jump.

Mary was standing in the doorway with a look of annoyance on her face. "Who have you been on the phone with for so long? I've been trying to call for over an hour," she sputtered. "I finally came by to make sure you're okay."

Once in the house, Mary spotted the phone and knew instantly why it was busy: the receiver was upside down and off kilter.

"Clara, your phone is off the hook. And it's upside down," she scolded her friend. "You really must be more careful. I was worried when I couldn't reach you."

"I can't understand why. For heaven's sake, you're so upset!" Clara said. "Anyone could've made that mistake. Just relax. I'll get you a cup of chamomile tea. Maybe it'll calm you down. Look at you, upset over nothing!"

"Clara, I can't stay right now," Mary said. "I'm waiting for an important phone call. I'll be back later this afternoon." Mary turned to leave, but noticed the dolls sitting on the couch. Clara followed her stare.

"How do you like my new family?" Clara asked her matter-of-factly. Mary turned to Clara, then back at the dolls. "Well, what do you think of my new friends?" Clara asked again.

"Well, I ... I think they're lovely, Clara."

"I found them in a trunk in the attic, banging to get out."

"You know, Clara, I think I *will* have a cup of tea after all. I want to hear more about these dolls. It sounds interesting." Mary got an earful.

Back home, Mary came up with the idea to invite Clara to dinner at five o'clock that same day. She wanted to hear more.

In the meantime, Clara found her sewing machine tucked in a corner of the closet. She decided she better ask Mary to help bring it downstairs when she came by again. Then she headed to the attic to find the box of patterns for doll dresses.

Halfway up the stairs, she heard the banging sound again. It grew louder the closer she got to the attic door. This time the sound was deafening; she put her hands to her ears to try to block out the noise. As she reached the top of the attic stairs, the banging stopped. She pushed open the attic door and glanced around. Where hadn't she looked? She noticed a small box tucked in a corner and headed straight for it. Inside, she found nothing but a beautiful, dark-brown teddy bear.

Gently she picked it up and pressed its small, soft body to her chest. "You belong with a family, not tucked away up here all by yourself in the attic." Clara then noticed that she couldn't hear the banging anymore, and that's when she realized that it was the teddy bear trying to get out of the box.

She decided to call it "Teddy." He reminded her of her favorite teddy bear her mother had given her as a child. She squeezed her prized possession close to her chest and kissed each cold black eye. Then she whispered in its ear, "I think of all the beautiful treasures I've found today, you're my favorite."

With Teddy cuddled in her arms, Clara found the patterns she was looking for and headed back downstairs.

∞

Later that day the phone rang, just as Clara finished ironing the last of the dolls' dresses. It was Mary reminding her about dinner.

At first Clara tried to wiggle her way out of having to go out; she didn't want to leave her new family. But Mary insisted; they hadn't had a meal together in quite a while, she reminded Clara.

"I'm told I make the best fish cakes in the nation," Mary wheedled, "and they taste better if you eat them the day they're made."

Clara reluctantly accepted the dinner invitation.

Chapter Thirteen

Best Friends Forever

MARY WAS GLAD SHE talked Clara into coming for a meal. She knew it would do her good to get out, and this would give her a chance to talk to Clara a little and see what was going on. The doll thing was totally strange, not a bit like Clara. She hoped she wasn't becoming demented.

She couldn't help wondering if some of Clara's forgetfulness might be due to all the stress she'd been under, caring for Frank all those months before he died, along with the grief and deep isolation that followed. It was remarkable how she stuck by him, waiting on him day and night. Towards the end, Robert spent more and more time helping too. Poor Darcy, on the other hand, couldn't bear to watch her father die, making up one excuse after another as to why she couldn't make it home. It hurt Clara to not have her daughter more involved, but she probably knew it just wasn't in Darcy's make-up.

Mary would do anything for Clara. After all, she was like a sister to her. She smiled as she thought back to the time when they were just children.

Miss Pray, their first-grade teacher, was as tall as she was plump. Rosy red cheeks and snow-white hair pulled up on top of her head made her look like Old Mother Goose; wire-rim glasses sitting snug on the bridge of her nose added to the illusion. Most of the time she looked over the top of them instead of through them.

On the first day of school Miss Pray asked each child, polished and clean, to make a circle around the room. It was a ritual of hers. The children counted off one, two, and then one, two again in succession, until each child was either a one or a two.

The ones were asked to choose their seats first, starting at the back and working toward the front of the class. Every child's eyes filled with a combination of excitement and nervousness. Then the twos found their seats amidst the ones.

By the time everyone was seated, the room was full of commotion. The tapping of Miss Pray's ruler on her large wooden desk was all that was required to bring instant silence to the room.

The sturdy oak desks comfortably accommodated two children. Clara and Mary found themselves desk mates. There are certain times in a person's life when fate steps in and connects two individuals. Sometimes it's for a short period of time, or it can be for a lifetime. Mary and Clara's friendship was sealed by fate on that first day of school—for a lifetime.

Mary was raised by a loving and determined family, making her a strong, unique individual and a trusting friend to Clara. The ingredients Mary was made from, blended with Clara's kindheartedness, made them kindred spirits. Mary knew there wasn't a mean part of Clara. She was kind and gentle-natured, almost to her disadvantage. Mary recalled the time that she accidentally broke one of Clara's mother's lead crystal water goblets. She had let it slip out of her hand while she was admiring it. Clara insisted that she should tell her mother it was she who broke it. She was afraid her mother would be so angry with Mary that she wouldn't allow her back into their house to play. So, Clara took the blame. Clara's mother's yelled at her and called her stupid and clumsy. Repeated berating like that from her mother caused Clara to develop into a timid child, which followed her into adulthood. As an adult, it was Frank who occasionally undermined her goodness. It took her years to learn to fight back and stick up for herself.

For as early as Mary could recall, it was her mother whom she always looked up to. Their relationship was different from the relationship Clara had with her own mother. Clara knew her mother loved her in her own way, but that she had difficulty showing it. While Clara's relationship was strained, Mary and her mother's relationship was built on love and trust. They were as close as a mother and daughter could be. Mary learned to stand up for what she believed in. Her courage won her the respect of her friends and acquaintances.

Mary would never forget the first incident as a young girl that convinced her that she wanted to be just like her mother. Mary smiled as she thought about the day, she came home from school with tears spilling down her tiny brown cheeks. One of the boys in her class had knocked her down and called her a stupid darkie. Mary would never forget her mother's response. "You know what I always say, Mary: sticks and stones may break your bones, but names will never hurt you. *However,* there *is* one time when you do have to fight," Fleta Thomas told her daughter with an understanding look. "When someone teases you because of the color of your skin."

The following day, Mary's mother was called to the principal's office because Mary had gotten into a fight with the same bully. Mary knocked him to the ground and hit him so hard he was afraid to get up.

Fleta, a tall, broad-shouldered woman who carried herself with poise and elegance, was neither aggressive nor passive. Both Mary and Fleta sat across from the principal, Mr. MacDonald, a short man with beady eyes and a shiny bald head. He asked Mary to tell him why she had gotten into the fight. When Mary shyly looked up at her mother and began to talk in a whisper, her mother nudged her to speak up.

"He called me a stupid darkie," Mary suddenly shouted. "My mother says if anyone calls me a name like that, I should fight." Fleta sat up straighter in her chair and cleared her throat, then gave Mary another half-smile and patted the top of her head. She was proud of her daughter for speaking up.

Then Fleta turned toward the principal, who was glaring at her as he tapped his pen rhythmically on his desk. It was clear he was indecisive about how he would handle the situation. "Is ... is what Mary said ... true?" he stammered.

Now it was Fleta's turn to glare at him. Curling her lip in anger, she replied, "Mary is telling the truth. I've taught her to never tell lies." Mary looked at her mother out of the corner of her eye, fearing the worst, and braced herself in the chair.

The principal stood up and came around his desk to face Fleta. Mary's little heart began to race. Then he held out his hand. Fleta stood up and accepted his handshake. "I'll see to it, Mrs. Thomas, that Mary doesn't get bothered again."

Mary's little body slowly sank deeper into the padded green, oversized chair in which she was sitting. She breathed a sigh of relief.

As she and her mother walked home hand-in-hand that day, it seemed to Mary, as she looked up at her mother, that she was the tallest, bravest lady she had ever seen.

Mary never looked for struggles or fights, yet she knew how much to hold her ground, that's for sure. She had her mother to thank for that.

Mary thought about Frank, remembering the early days of Clara's marriage to him. She'd had a cordial relationship with him, although he wasn't much of a talker; it was up to her to strike up a conversation with him about this or that. She knew all about his and Clara's strained relationship. She felt, as Clara did, that things would have been different if he hadn't suffered from depression. She and Frank would talk briefly about the weather or about something in the news, then she'd leave him to enjoy his television programs.

Clara and Mary had plenty to talk about in Clara's kitchen, or Mary's, over a cup of coffee or tea. The most Frank ever talked was when Mary got sick and had to quit her job as a nurse. Mary could tell he was genuinely concerned about her health.

Dr. Hoyt finally diagnosed Mary with fatigue, but he never found any explanation as to why she was so debilitated. It made no sense to Mary that at her age she was so tired all the time. She had no energy to do even simple chores around the house, never mind go to work. She consulted with a Naturopathic physician and read books on nutrition, supplements, stress reduction techniques, and related matters.

She spent a lot of money on supplements and organic foods, becoming acutely conscious of what foods she should eat and not eat. It took her almost a year, but she was finally able to heal herself. Dr. Hoyt admitted that he didn't know what to do for her, and actually was surprisingly pleased with Mary's holistic approach to her health.

Frank couldn't believe the change in her feeling better. He asked questions now and then about the natural things she did for herself. He admired her for what she did. When he got sick, his doctor told him to go home and prepare to die. That's when he asked for Mary's help. He knew Mary was knowledgeable in holistic health. She was not a doctor, but she knew enough to get him feeling better. Eventually Frank made the decision on his own to see the Naturopathic doctor Mary had gone to, who helped strengthen him to the end of his life. He felt he had nothing to lose since he was going to die anyway. Mary recalled telling him the most important change he could make in his life was to put away negative thoughts.

Mary and Frank grew close those last few months of his life. It gave him some peace to be able to unburden his heart. He knew Mary wouldn't be judgmental. Any private information he shared with her was safe. Mary still cherished the moments when he would confide in her. Once he poured his heart out to her about what it was like to live with depression.

Mary continued setting the table for dinner. She went to the corner cupboard for water glasses, her mind deep in thought about Frank's heart-wrenching story. She stared into space, remembering that awful day...

The Vietnam War had drastically changed Frank's life. He'd been living with a story no one, not even Clara, knew about. He never could bring himself to talk about it.

One day in the middle of the night, six guys, including Frank, were in a foxhole. They hadn't slept or eaten in days. They were being assaulted with machine-gun fire and bombs all day and night.

Everyone was afraid. No one thought they were going to get out alive.

Each person's struggle was a living hell. No one talked about their fear, trying hard to be brave for the next guy. The smell of dead flesh was in the air. Their army uniforms were soiled with mud and infested with bodily fluids, including blood. Then it happened. They got hit—a grenade landed square inside the foxhole. Everyone was killed instantly except for Frank and Sergeant Moore, who was barely alive. He had a gaping leg wound. There was nothing Frank could do for him.

He had no medicine.

He held the sergeant in his arms for hours. He was in and out of consciousness. When he was conscious, he begged Frank to kill him, his pain was so intolerable. Frank kept shaking his head—he didn't want to do it. While the sergeant was conscious Frank asked him if he believed in God. Sergeant Moore said he did. Frank told him what he believed to be true. "Don't be afraid of dying," he told him. "No one ever dies, we go back to our heavenly home where there is no pain or sorrow." Then Sergeant Moore started screaming in agony. Frank knew if he didn't kill him, he'd be a dead man too, an easy target for the enemy.

Frank gritted his teeth; his eyes were stinging with tears. He couldn't look the sergeant in the eyes when he did the unspeakable, so he rolled him onto his stomach. He took his rifle in hand, aimed it at his head, and then he pulled the trigger. Frank watched the sergeant's body jerk and quiver for a few moments, then it was over.

Frank had to put his hands tight against his mouth to keep himself from screaming. At times, long after the war, he'd wake up in a cold sweat, tortured by nightmares. He never forgave himself for what he had to do. For years he wished it had been the other way around, that he was the one who died.

Mary shook herself to bring herself back to the present. But her thoughts stayed with Frank. She went back to the cabinet to get some napkins. Frank told her he felt sorry for the way his relationship with his family had changed after the war. He knew it was because of his depression. He felt it was too late to undo the wrong he had done to Clara. He felt like a damaged man.

Mary placed a pair of white napkins by each place setting, then stopped again, deep in thought. One day, just before he died, he was rambling. "I forgave her, Mary," he said.

"You forgave her for what, Frank?" she recalled asking him, but she didn't want to pry. After all, it was something between the two of them. Frank stopped rambling, and then he fell asleep. She never knew what he forgave Clara for. Mary shook her head, still puzzled after all this time. She headed back into the kitchen to check on what she was cooking, but with her mind still on Frank.

During the last few weeks he had left, he and Mary liked to talk about life after death. It was a subject he knew Mary was interested in. He thanked her for everything she had done for him. He was happy for the devotion she had shown his family, especially Clara. He looked her in the eye, blew her a kiss, then winked. "I'm ready to end my journey, Mary, and thanks to you, I'm not afraid to die." She was touched by his words.

Chapter Fourteen

More Causes for Concern

MARY HAD KNOWN FOR years that there was a well-kept secret between Clara and Frank, but she never knew what it was; it was none of her business. A few days after Frank passed away, Mary recalled visiting Clara. She could see she had been crying. They sat in her living room and the silence was terrible. She couldn't take it another minute. She asked Clara if she needed to talk.

Clara took a Kleenex from her pocket and blew her nose, then nodded. Yes, she wanted to talk. Now that Frank was gone, she needed to let a hidden secret out of the bag.

Mary took Clara's hand in hers. "Let it out, honey. Take all the time you need."

Clara took a deep breath and, with red and swollen eyes, started to tell Mary her secret—then stopped. "No," she decided, "I can't talk about it right now, Mary. Maybe some other time, when I am not so upset, I can share it with you."

Mary didn't want to force Clara to talk. She wanted her to be comfortable talking about whatever the secret was. She wondered if it had anything to do with what Frank had said to her, about forgiving her. She thought it must be something that had been eating away at her for a long time. Once she could talk about it, she knew she'd feel like a huge weight had been lifted off her shoulders. She'd been carrying Mount Everest for long enough. But Clara just couldn't talk about whatever was bothering her, at least not yet.

Mary reminisced about the many meals she'd had with them when the kids were young. Clara would cook a nice big dinner and run around waiting on her family, making sure that everyone was fed and happy, never thinking of herself. By the time she sat down to eat, everyone else had eaten, but that didn't bother her a bit. It bothered Mary whenever she was invited to eat with them, but she learned after a while to keep her mouth shut and just eat.

With Clara, it was family first. *No wonder the poor woman had an evening cocktail. She needed it,* Mary mused. The children were a blessing to her. Of course, they were spoiled. When the children had a problem, it was Clara they ran to. When they were sick, it was Clara who nursed them back to health. She took them to all their activities and never missed a game they played in. Robert had his baseball and basketball, and Darcy had her dance lessons.

Once, when Robert was just a baby, there was a big northeaster. The snow was so high they couldn't open the doors, front or back. Frank hurt his back trying to shovel the snow. Clara nursed him back to health, but it was two months before Frank was able to return to work. Mary went over on weekends for a few hours just to give Clara a break, and made herself available to Clara if she needed to run errands during the week as well. Frank could only complain about anything she tried to do for him. The food wasn't hot enough. Why couldn't she keep the children quiet when he was trying to sleep?

That was a long time ago, and Mary would still do anything for Clara and the children. They were family to her.

Mary let her eyes glance around the living room of her own home. Clara was due in an hour, and she was pleased with how everything looked. She had always admired the charming architecture of the old house. The ceilings were tall with beautiful crown moldings in every room. The living room had always been her favorite room in the house. The big windows let in a lot of light.

The walls in all the downstairs rooms were painted off-white. She had decorated those rooms with colorful curtains and lots of art for the walls. She glanced over at one of her favorite paintings, an oil painting of her house, which hung over the fireplace. It was a gift to her mother from a friend of hers, a well-known artist in South Port. She had always admired the way the artist had depicted the exterior of their home with such detail and skill.

The beautiful antique colonial had deep-green shutters on either side of all its large windows. The screened-in porch at one end of the house was always the family's favorite place to sit on hot summer nights and autumn days. The room on the other side of the house was called the winter room. It had floor-to-ceiling windows on three sides. In the winter the sun would flood the room, warming it on cold afternoons.

Mary loved the dark-mahogany oval mirror at the far end of the room. It was one of her favorite pieces of Grandmother Flower's. Mary was too young to remember much about her grandmother. She did remember how much she loved her though. She had clear memories of being cared for by her when her mother was working. She remembered how much she loved spending time with her alone, just the two of them. They had a special link.

Standing in the dining room, she admired how pretty the table looked. A cut-glass vase with red and white carnations sat in the center of the white tablecloth. Her favorite china, crystal, and silverware gleamed. She was not one to save her good things for Sunday dinner.

Mary knew Clara wasn't doing much cooking these days. Once the kids were out of the house, and then after Frank died, she lost her desire to cook. She knew how Clara felt because she wasn't fond of eating alone either, but she never let it bother her. It made no sense to dwell on something that couldn't be changed.

Glancing at the wall clock in the kitchen, she realized it was a little past five. Clara should be here any minute now. She went into the living room, put on some soft music, then returned to the kitchen. Reaching up to the kitchen cabinet, she brought down two wine glasses and set them on a tray. When Clara arrived, they'd both have a little sherry before dinner.

By 5:15, Mary started to wonder where she was. She began to worry that something was wrong, and telephoned. After the third ring, Clara answered.

"Hi, Clara. Are you on your way?" Mary asked.

"On my way where, Mary?" Clara sounded genuinely mystified.

"I invited you over here for dinner." The silence told Mary that Clara had forgotten. "Don't you remember, dear?"

There was another long pause at the other end of the line, and then Clara spoke. "I'm … I'm so sorry, Mary. What time was I supposed to be there?"

"It doesn't matter," Mary said as cheerfully as she could. "Just get here as soon as you can, before the food gets cold."

"Okay, honey, I'll just change my clothes. I was ironing some doll clothes for my friends. I'll put things away and come right over."

Mary hung up the phone. *What on earth is up with Clara? Oh, maybe I shouldn't be so alarmed. Anyone can forget … but ironing doll clothes?*

Mary was just about ready to let the whole incident go when Clara showed up at her back door—with three dolls and a teddy bear tucked neatly in a basket.

Chapter Fifteen

These Are Not Ordinary Dolls

TRYING HER HARDEST NOT to look surprised, Mary eyed each doll, then looked up at Clara and asked, "Well, who are your friends?"

Clara proudly introduced them to Mary. "This is Sarah, this is Frances, and this is Baby. And this," she said, smiling at the bear, "is Teddy, of course."

Sitting in the living room, as they sipped their before-dinner sherry, Mary decided to test Clara's memory. "Clara, do you remember my Grandmother Flower?"

"Oh, yes," Clara answered, not taking her eyes off her dolls as she continued to fuss over them.

Mary got up and went over to the hutch and took out her old family album. Then she walked over and sat down on the sofa next to Clara, who said to the dolls, "Move over and let's give our Mary a little room." Clara gently pushed the dolls over to make a place for Mary to sit.

Mary turned the album pages to a picture of her grandmother. "My mother always said I looked like my Grandmother Flower. Do you think I look like her?"

Clara stopped occupying herself with the dolls, gave Mary a long, serious look, then finally said, "You know, Mary, I do believe you do. I never realized it until now."

"I was too small to remember much about my grandmother," Mary continued. "I do remember how much I loved her though. I know she took care of me when Mother was working. I loved our alone time, just the two of us. I remember when I was a baby, she and Granddaddy Flower brought me all the goat's milk that I could drink. Weak stomach is what the doctor said I had. It was Grandmother Flower who bought me my first dog. Grandmother convinced Mother that I should grow up with a pet, so she bought me Buster. Buster went with us everywhere we could take him. Do you remember Buster, Clara?"

"Actually, no, I don't, dear," Clara admitted.

"The only place Buster didn't go was to school." Mary had to chuckle. "Once he did follow us to school and the principal had to call Mother to come for him. Mother was angry as a hornet that she had to stop what she was doing to come and get him. I'll never forget. She showed up, lips tight and curled into a frown, like she used to when she was really mad, with leash in hand. She took him home. After that, Buster wasn't allowed to go out until we'd left for school. Surely you remember Buster, Clara."

"Was he a big black dog?" Clara asked as she wrinkled her nose, as if the gesture would help her remember.

"No," Mary said, annoyed that she didn't remember. "He was a yellow lab. Don't you recall? You loved him as much as anyone."

"No, I guess I've forgotten." Clara didn't seem particularly concerned.

Mary continued on with her reminiscences. "It was my grandmother who took me to church for the very first time. Mother didn't enforce that church-going business. She said there were more sinners in the church than out. When Grandmother got through with Mother, she never said another word about us going to church."

Clara laughed. "I do remember your mother. She was nice."

"Once in a while Mother would go with Grandmother and me to church. One Sunday the pastor was standing tall and preaching loud from the pulpit about people changing their evil ways. He was talking about people who went out on Saturday nights drinking and acting the fool, then would come to church on Sunday acting all high and mighty. He said they couldn't get into the Kingdom of Heaven. Sitting next to Mother I heard her say under her breath so Grandmother couldn't hear her that if he didn't mind his own business he couldn't get into the kingdom either."

Both Clara and Mary had a good belly laugh. "Our families have been around here for years," Mary chuckled, "and being as I am one of a few of us folks, I'm proud I brought some color to the neighborhood."

"I'm glad we at least have a good size population of black people in our town, and of course enough to fill our church."

Mary glanced over at Clara. She had finally stopped fumbling with the dolls. Now suddenly she had a distressed, far away look on her face.

"Clara, is anything the matter?" Mary asked with concern. "You looked so sad just then."

"I'm ... I'm fine. I was just thinking of Dave for a moment," Clara admitted.

"I'm hungry," Clara announced briskly, changing the subject "Let's eat."

Mary laughed. "I guess I better check on dinner then," she said. I'll be right back. Just relax and enjoy your cocktail."

Mary went into the kitchen to check on dinner. Glancing into the living room on her way to the refrigerator, she stopped in her tracks. She couldn't help listening to Clara talking to the dolls, fussing over them like they were real.

"Lord, what in the world is happening to Clara?" she whispered to herself, shaking her head in disbelief. Then she recalled how just the mention of Dave's name had caused her friend to look so sad. Mary was sincerely concerned. *I wonder what is happening to poor Clara. I'm going to have to get nosey and start asking some questions at dinner. I need to get to the bottom of this.*

The dolls sat on the chair next to Clara at the dinner table. It was as plain as the nose on Mary's face that Clara was in trouble. Did she really believe these dolls were real? As they sat at the table having their meal, Mary decided that it was time to confront her.

Taking a long, slow breath, she began. "Clara, I was going to mention something to you when you came to dinner today. I couldn't help but notice the doll clothes on your clothesline on my way back home after seeing you this morning. And now you've brought the dolls along with you. Well, I do have to say I'm sort of, surprised." Finally, she just blurted it out. "What's up, Clara? Why are you talking to them as if they're real?"

Clara put down her fork and finished chewing the food in her mouth. Mary could almost see the wheels turning in her head. "Well, they're as real as you or me," Clara said firmly. "Isn't this wonderful, Mary?

These are my new friends. I found them in the attic. They have been trying for weeks to get my attention."

"Get your attention," Mary almost shrieked.

"They need me as much as I need them," Clara continued calmly. "Mary, I have to ask you a favor. I want to keep what I am about to tell you just between the two of us, dear. I'll surprise Darcy and Robert myself when the time comes."

"Don't you think it's a little odd, walking around with dolls at your age?"

Clara suddenly turned on her friend. "You don't understand, Mary," she said angrily. "These are no ordinary dolls."

"What can you possibly mean, Clara, no ordinary dolls?" Mary was practically at her wit's end.

"Okay," Clara said peevishly, I'll get to the point. I kept hearing sounds, like pounding or sometimes singing, but for days I couldn't figure out where it was coming from. Then yesterday, just before you came over, I had the idea to go up into the attic, and sure enough when I opened up the trunk, there they were— lots and lots of dolls and teddy bears and stuffed animals. I'm sure they must belong to the children, but for the life of me, I can't remember them having so many of them," Clara said, shaking her head.

"Anyway, once I got the ones I wanted downstairs, I realized that the banging sounds had stopped. And they stayed stopped. They were just trying to get out, Mary. You see, they needed me as much as I needed them."

"What do you mean, they needed you?" Mary asked, trying to keep the fear that was growing in her out of her voice. "Since when do dolls and stuffed animals need people?"

"That's what I am trying to tell you, Mary," Clara said patiently. "They aren't just ordinary dolls and stuffed animals. They're real."

Mary closed her eyes and looked away from Clara, then took a big swallow of water. *Lord have mercy, I can't believe what I am hearing.*

When she opened her eyes and turned back to face her friend, Clara was eating her meal and talking to one of the dolls with an expression of pure joy and contentment. Clara looked so happy.

Mary wondered again if she was getting demented. If that was the case, she knew she couldn't convince her something was very wrong with her. She wondered how she could help.

One thing was for sure, Robert and Darcy were going to have to know about their mother. "Clara," Mary said gently, breaking the silence, "when are you going to surprise the children?" Before Clara could answer, Mary added, "I think you should call them tonight."

"No, not tonight," Clara said quickly, "Darcy may come up this weekend. I'll wait till then so she can see for herself. Then she'll understand how special they are. Don't you think they're wonderful, Mary?"

Mary found herself at a loss for words, but she still had to ask one very important question. "Clara," she finally said, with the feeling of a lump growing in her throat, "do the dolls and stuffed animals talk?"

Mary held her breath for the answer, hoping that Clara would say, "Of course not, silly!" But to her surprise, she answered matter-of-factly, "They understand everything I say to them, dear. That's what makes them so special."

Mary repeated the question. "Clara," she said, her heart racing, "now think about this. Do they talk? Do they *really* talk?"

"Only to me," Clara answered.

Overcome with sadness, Mary wished with all her heart that she had not heard that answer. The lump in her throat and her chest muscles tightened. It was hardly the answer she wanted. Clara was in trouble and she had to help her, but how?

They finished the meal in silence: Mary too saddened by what she had just seen and heard, and Clara too amused with her new friends and too confused to see the seriousness of the situation. Once the meal was over, Clara helped Mary clear off the table. Then they decided to sit in the living room by the fire to have their cup of coffee.

Mary had hoped to find another opportunity to ask Clara a few more questions about her new friends, and why just the mention of Dave's name had made her look so extremely sad. But before she could, the phone rang. She excused herself and went into the kitchen to answer the phone. It was Darcy.

Darcy shared with Mary that she was relieved to know her mother was not only finally out of the house, but that she was having dinner with her. She and Robert had been worried about their mother living alone. They would feel different if she were out socializing and enjoying herself instead of sitting home alone. They felt the truth was she was slowly becoming a recluse and was downplaying the fact that she was having a difficult time adjusting to being alone. Darcy insisted that Mary not disturb her. She asked Mary to tell her mother she would call her later. Mary didn't tell Darcy about the dolls, but she planned to tell her and Robert soon.

After hanging up the phone and before returning to the living room, Mary took a long, deep breath, arched her shoulders, and adjusted her neck from side to side, closing her eyes for a few minutes as she took in more deep breaths and let them out gently. With each breath in and out she could feel her tense body relax a little bit more. She had been doing yoga every morning for many years and it worked; she knew how to relieve tension in her body when she needed to.

Chapter Sixteen

An Attempt at Diverting the Unusual

MARY WANTED TO GET a better handle on what was going on with Clara. Then she would have something to tell Robert and Darcy. Clara's losing her driver's license, talking to stuffed animals and dolls, forgetting dinner engagements, and not putting the phone correctly on the hook all indicated possible serious mental problems. But she didn't want to be blowing it all out of proportion, either.

Taking in one more deep breath, Mary walked back into the living room. Clara looked almost too peaceful to disturb. She had dozed off to sleep with her newfound friends, the dolls and Teddy, on her lap. Mary walked over to her and gently tapped her on the shoulder.

Clara woke up instantly with a startled look.

While they sat comfortably next to each other on the couch having coffee, Mary told Clara that Darcy had called while she was snoozing. Clara was disappointed that she missed her call, but was glad to know Darcy would call later. Clara thought it was sweet that Darcy didn't want to disturb her evening with Mary. She knew sometimes Darcy could be thoughtful when she wanted to. During the course of their conversation, it became clear to Mary that Clara had no recollection of when she had seen Darcy last, or Robert either for that matter. Clara had to admit that time was going way too fast for her and she couldn't seem to remember when the children's visits were. The only thing she was certain of was what a joy her new friends were to her, she revealed to Mary, as she smiled down at her basket of dolls and stuffed animals.

Clara lifted up her coffee cup and took a long sip before putting the cup back on its saucer, then sat back and folded her hands in her lap to give her full attention to Mary. She knew Mary wanted to spend more time together.

Mary insisted they weren't getting any younger, and she missed spending time with her. She admitted it was really her fault—she'd been so preoccupied with herself. Monday and Wednesday and Friday she went to the community center, her favorite activity being chair yoga. She also volunteered at the hospital

Tuesday afternoons. Thursday was her free day, "and to tell you the truth," she said, "I'm so tired by Thursday, I try not to do one single thing." Mary asked Clara if she would like to join the community center.

Clara started to laugh before Mary could continue. "I'm busy myself with my friends. I don't think so!"

Mary was ready for the objection. She explained it was the senior yoga class instructor who told her that a lot of women their age who go to the center enjoy the yoga class. "One woman couldn't put on pantyhose when she started, and now she can put them on standing up!"

"Well, good for her, but, no, I don't think I would like it, not now anyway. Besides, I don't wear pantyhose anymore."

Mary wasn't going to be so easily defeated. She suggested some volunteer work at the hospital.

Clara folded her arms. "The only time I want to go to a hospital is kicking and screaming."

"Okay, Clara, what would you like to do?" Mary asked, exasperated.

"I've got plenty to do. I'm keeping myself busy these days with my friends."

"That, dear, is my point. You're too busy with 'your friends.' I'm trying to help you to see how important it is for you to get out of the house more, to be with people."

"It's too cold to go out now," Clara said, sounding entirely practical. "And besides, I don't like driving in this weather. You never know when we could have a freak snowstorm."

"Clara, you can't drive anymore; you lost your license after you got stopped by a policeman. And besides that, you shouldn't have been driving without a license. You lost it after the accident, remember?"

"What accident?" Clara looked genuinely puzzled.

"When you backed into the tree," Mary reminded her. "Thank goodness no one was hurt. You said the sun was in your eyes and you couldn't see."

"I must talk to Robert about helping me get it back," Clara said. "Since my cataract was removed, I can see fine."

"Clara, you know I'll drive you wherever you want to go."

"I know you will, but I want to drive myself," Clara said stubbornly.

"But for now, Clara, until you can get it back, if you get it back, I'll drive you. So, what excuse can you think up now?" Mary knew she finally had her cornered. She wasn't sure she wanted to hear what excuse Clara was going to produce.

Clara could see from the look on Mary's face that she was getting annoyed with her. She told her she wished she could spend more time with her, and she promised to sometime soon, but for now she just couldn't leave her new friends for long periods of time.

Mary's lips began to flatten out into a tight line of frustration. Stopping herself, she redirected them into a gentle smile, took a deep breath, and softly reached out. Taking both of Clara's hands in hers and looking into her friend's pretty, sky-blue eyes, she said, "The dolls and teddy bears are not real, dear Clara."

"You're wrong, Mary," Clara said in a voice cold with disappointment. "They *are* real. They're *very* real, to me anyway, and that's all that matters. I should think you, of all people, would be happy for me. As for Darcy and Robert, that will take some getting used to for them. Young people have their own set ideas about what they think widowed mothers should be doing. But you, of all people, should understand, Mary."

Clara sat quiet for a moment. Then she added, "They make me happy, Mary. They're my friends. The house is so empty without them. Try to see my point."

Chapter Seventeen

A Handshake Seals the Deal

MARY CAME UP WITH the idea that both of them had to give a little to make this work. They decided on a plan to go shopping and out to lunch every Saturday. Clara was reluctant at first, but then agreed. She didn't have the heart to disappoint Mary. She also knew she would have to give up something. She knew her friend was persistent.

"So, is that a deal, then?" Mary asked, her hand outstretched.

"Deal," said Clara. The handshake sealed it. "Now, I'm ready to go home. I'm tired, Mary."

Clara bundled herself up for the weather and headed for the door, then hurried back to get the basket of dolls she had carefully packed. She had nearly forgotten them.

Mary stood at the open door and watched Clara make her way across the backyard. An almost-full moon shining down through the trees gave Clara just enough light to see the shoveled, well-traveled path through the snow that led to her own back door.

Clara looked like a small bundle, dressed in her light-brown peacoat and matching hat, her basket tucked over her arm. Walking slowly, she made little footprints in the snow as she planted each foot carefully and securely. As soon as she reached the steps, she turned and waved to Mary.

Mary closed the door and walked into the kitchen to finish cleaning up, deep in thought over the evening. A few moments later, she was startled by a knock at the door.

Dish in hand, she went to the door. To her surprise, there was Clara standing on her doorstep, her dolls huddled close.

"What's wrong, Clara? Did you forget something?" she asked.

"I can't find my key," Clara said, nearly crying in frustration.

Mary smiled, went to a drawer in the kitchen, and took out a spare key to Clara's house. "Here you go," she said. "Return it when you find your set, okay?"

The two friends embraced again, and Clara shuffled back over to her house. Mary watched her from the doorway and made sure she got inside.

Chapter Eighteen

A Hint Almost Lets the Cat Out of the Bag

CLARA ENTERED HER HOUSE. The warmth of it brought immediate comfort to her bones, though the cold evening air that followed her in made her shiver.

"Well, Teddy, Sarah, Frances, and Baby, it's nice to go out," she said, while taking off her coat, scarf, hat, and gloves, "but even nicer to come home, don't you think?" She took the dolls out of the basket and placed them side by side on the couch next to her chair.

She decided to sit for a minute and relax while watching the television before heading upstairs to bed. She snuggled into her slippers, which she kept tucked neatly under the coffee table. She felt comfortable and content in her little home. She glanced over at the dolls and smiled. She knew they had a good time too. She winked at Teddy—he was her favorite.

She imagined them all nodding yes in unison.

The next thing she knew, the ringing of the telephone woke her from a deep sleep.

"Hello," she said, clearing her throat.

"Hi, Mom," came Darcy's voice. "Did I wake you?"

"Actually, yes. I guess I must have dozed off. What time is it, honey?"

"Eight thirty. Did I call too late?"

"No, but dear me, I slept though my television program," Clara acknowledged.

"Did you have a good time?"

"A good time where, dear?"

"At Mary's house," Darcy said, surprised. "You were there for a visit when I called. I'd tried you at home first. When you didn't answer, I called over to Mary's. Didn't she tell you that I called?"

"I'm sure she must have and I just forgot," Clara admitted.

"I told her to tell you I'd call later." Darcy decided not to dwell on it. "I was so happy you finally got out of the house," she said, in an attempt to inject some enthusiasm into the conversation.

"Yes, we enjoyed ourselves. We're going shopping and out to eat on Saturday. Or Thursday—I am not sure which day."

"Why, that's great, Mom!" she approved. "I'm so happy that you're starting to get out of the house more. It'll do you good. You know I've been trying to get you to go out more, ever since Dad passed away. See now, don't you feel much better getting out?"

"Yes, you are right, dear," Clara said automatically. "It is good to get out. But you know, sometimes people have to do things at their own pace."

"I don't mean to be pushy, Mom," Darcy back-pedaled. "I just worry about you sometimes."

Darcy then decided to try her luck and asked her mother if she'd thought anymore about going to the senior center.

"No, and I am not going to think about it, either," Clara stated firmly. "I told you, I don't want to go there. It's just not for me. I don't belong in those places with people who are old and confused."

Darcy decided not to argue with her and was about to start talking about something else, but Clara continued in a tone of voice Darcy was used to when her mother was upset or wanted to make a point.

"I think it was Dotty who told me she stopped going there because there was this one woman there, I think her name was Katie and she'd walk around in these tight pants. Her pants were so tight you could see she was wearing Depends. To make matters worse, she wore these god-awful, huge, cheap earrings that dangled almost down to her shoulders." Clara was on a roll. "And she keeps repeating herself over and over, 'Does anyone know where Mother is? Has anyone seen my mother?' Great company she'd be. I know I forget things once in a while, but I'm not nearly as bad off as those poor, demented souls. I am *not* ready for the rocking chair, Darcy."

Darcy tried to calm her mother down. She assured her that her whole point in mentioning the center was for her mother to make new friends to keep from feeling lonely.

"Well, as a matter of fact, I don't feel lonely anymore!" Clara stopped herself before telling Darcy about her new family.

"Are you keeping something from me, Mom? Do you have new friends?"

Clara smiled to herself as she glanced over at the dolls sitting together on the couch, their eyes fixed and their mouths turned up in the most pleasant smiles.

"You'll meet them when you come to visit," Clara said.

"Oh, there's more than one? That's terrific!"

Clara was pleased to know Darcy planned to come for a visit in a few weeks, even though Darcy couldn't give her an exact date. Now that she had two families, she would never feel alone again.

Chapter Nineteen

Too Much Happening, Too Fast

CLARA TRIED NOT TO worry over the children too much, but she guessed most mothers did that sometimes. She wished Darcy would settle down and get married, raise a nice family, and stop all this traveling around. Clara felt the poor girl was missing out on the best part of life. She felt her daughter wouldn't fuss over her if she had her own family to worry about.

But now she wanted to see what the dolls and Teddy were up to. She needed to get them ready for bed. The idea of bed sounded good to her. It had been a long day, but a good one.

Slowly climbing each stair seemed like a chore, each stair seeming harder to climb than the one before it. Hanging onto the railing with both hands, she ascended, pausing now and then to catch her breath. Once at the top of the stairs, she sighed in relief. "I made it," she said aloud, but she felt exhausted. She never had this much trouble climbing the stairs before. She felt more tired than she could ever remember.

Taking short, slow steps, she made her way down the hall, running her hand along the wall for security until she got to her bedroom. Reaching out for the bedpost with both hands, she turned and sat on the bed, short of breath, her face pale and flushed. She grabbed hold of her chest with both hands.

Fear gripped her. It felt like something heavy was sitting on her chest. *God, I hope I'm not having a heart attack,* she thought. Fumbling for the phone on the bedside table, she called Mary. She glanced at the clock. It was 9:00 p.m. *She should still be awake. I know she doesn't usually go to bed till ten.*

Her hands were shaking as she dialed the number and waited while it rang. When Mary hadn't picked up after the second ring, panic began to creep through her mind. On the third ring, Mary answered.

"Hello."

"Mary, this is Clara. I am feeling poorly and I hated to call, but ..."

Mary cut her short. "What is it, Clara? Are you alright?

"Well, no," Clara had to admit. "I'm having chest pains."

"Hang up the phone," Mary said instantly. "I'll dial 911 and then I'll be right over." Clara did as she was instructed.

Mary dialed 911 and supplied the necessary information, then put on her coat and headed for her back door. Her hand on the doorknob, she groaned, remembering that she'd given Clara her extra key. *How am I going to get in her house with no key? Well, if I have to, I'll just break the damn window,* Mary thought with determination.

Walking as fast as she could, she took extra care not to slip and fall on the snow. This was no time for further complications. Once she reached Clara's back door, she decided to try it before breaking the glass. To her amazement, the door opened easily. Clara had forgotten to lock the door. For once Mary was glad of her friend's poor memory.

"I hope I am not going to die," Clara said out loud. Closing her eyes, she tried not to worry about dying, or anything else for that matter. She just concentrated on her breathing. Slow breaths in and slow breaths out.

Mary found Clara upstairs in her bedroom, lying down on her bed, looking like she'd fallen asleep. Tiptoeing quietly, she came in the room.

Hearing a slight noise beside her, Clara opened her eyes to find Mary smiling down at her. But through the smile, she also saw a look of concern on Mary's face.

"Oh, stop worrying," Clara grumbled. "I feel better already. Did you call 911?"

"Of course I called. They'll be here any minute." Mary pulled up a chair close to Clara's bed and took hold of her hand. Stroking it gently, she said, "You're going to be okay, honey."

"I know," Clara said agreeably. "I'm too stubborn to die."

Before Clara knew it, she was being whisked off to the hospital with sirens blaring into the night air.

Mary was beside herself with worry and concern for her friend. She couldn't bear the thought of losing her.

The last thing Clara said to Mary was to ask her to take good care of Baby, Frances, Teddy, and Sarah. Mary reassured her they were all going to be fine. She tried to get her to relax and not worry about a thing.

Mary called Robert and told him she was at the hospital with his mother, who was having chest pains and was being examined. She told him Clara was awake, that the doctor and nurses were taking care of her, and that they were definitely keeping her in the hospital this time.

It was time for Darcy and Robert to come home. There were some things going on with Clara that they needed to know. Mary was trying to wait until they both came in a few weeks, but now it couldn't wait— too much had happened too fast.

Chapter Twenty

A Serious Illness Threatens Health

THE NEXT DAY, ROBERT spent time visiting with his mother in the hospital. To everyone's relief, Clara was going to be alright, but she wasn't out of the woods. Robert had never seen his mother look so meek. All he wanted to do was to take care of her, protect her, and love her.

Later on that evening, Mary joined Robert and Darcy at their mother's house. Fearing the worst, they sat on the sofa across from Mary anxiously waiting to hear what Mary had to tell them about what had been going on with their mother. A fire crackled in the fireplace. It felt good; it was a cold evening. The coffee they were all drinking warmed them.

Robert was ready to hear what Mary had to tell him, but he knew it wouldn't be pleasant. However, before she could begin, Darcy spoke up. She had just noticed the dolls and Teddy sitting in a basket in a chair in the far corner of the room.

"Say, Mary, do you have any idea what all those dolls and stuffed animals are doing in the living room?" she asked, puzzled. "I thought Mother had given them all away years ago."

"Well," Mary began with a sigh, "that's part of what I have to talk to you about. I ... I am so worried about your mother." Mary took another deep breath and folded her hands together on her lap to keep them from shaking.

Mary told them that Clara had been hearing banging sounds in the house on a regular basis. This had been going on for weeks, maybe longer, Mary wasn't sure about the time, but the noises were becoming a nuisance. They would start in the morning and continue throughout the day, sometimes waking her up.

Darcy looked over at Robert, perplexed. Mary could see how surprised they both were by what she was telling them. She hated to have to frighten them, but she had no choice. It was time that they knew what was going on.

"On some occasions, it wasn't just banging your mother was hearing; once she heard someone calling her name. It all began to annoy her because it wouldn't stop." Mary paused to get a sip of coffee before plowing on.

"She finally decided to go up to the attic one day, thinking the sounds were coming from there. Heaven only knows why, but she'd searched the entire house, and it was the last place to look. That's when she found some of your old stuffed animals, Darcy, and dolls. She brought them down from the attic, cleaned them up, and even gave them names."

"Names?" Darcy repeated, trying to make sense of what she was hearing.

"The names worried me enough," she continued, "but what frightened me more was that she talked with them, and took them everywhere she went, even to my house when she came to dinner. And when she told me they talked back to her, I became alarmed."

Mary went on nonstop about all she'd seen and heard over the past few weeks. Then she produced the note concerning the medicine she had found in Clara's bathrobe pocket. "This may be the cause of some of Clara's confusion." She produced the note. Robert studied it for a moment.

Robert could see the misspelled words, but if she stopped all her meds, which he thought happened, he knew it could explain his mother's confusion. Robert handed the note over to Darcy, who read it.

Robert and Darcy sat looking at each other, stunned and speechless, hardly able to absorb all that was happening. It felt like a personal horror movie. They had no idea things had gotten so out of hand.

Robert and Darcy sat in silence, trying to make sense of everything they were hearing.

Robert finally broke his silence. "But ... I was here visiting with her a few weeks ago. She didn't say anything about banging then."

Mary explained to Robert that Clara didn't want either of them to know because she was afraid they'd think she wasn't capable of taking care of herself and she didn't want to be sent to a nursing home.

Robert shook his head slowly, trying to sort everything out in his mind. When he finally spoke, there was a crack in his voice, as if he was going to cry. He cleared his throat. "I've heard of this happening to older people when they become isolated and lonely. They drift into a world of make-believe."

"But Mom's not lonely," Darcy protested. "She has us, and Mary's right next door. And she just told me last night she has some new friends ..." Darcy's glance fell on the basket and her hand came to her mouth. "Are those her new friends?"

Mary nodded sadly.

"She *is* alone, Darcy," Robert said. "We're not here with her. Just being able to call us is hardly companionship."

"That's right, Darcy," Mary said quietly.

Robert said he would give Dr. Hoyt a call and tell him about the miscommunication about her medications. He would also ask the doctor if he could come to a family meeting the next day at the hospital where they could all discuss the matter further.

Both Mary and Darcy hoped Robert had some idea of what was going on with Clara. They were frightened, and needed to hear some explanation. Trying not to think the worst was difficult. Robert told them that his first thought was that she had a serious heart condition. But he wanted to leave the diagnosis up to Gus Hoyt, the expert when it comes to the heart. He also wanted his mother to be seen by a geropsychologist.

Darcy sat back in her chair, perplexed, then asked, "You're a doctor. Why can't *you* rule out dementia?"

"I'm not an expert in that field, Darcy. I want her to be seen by someone who works with this kind of thing all the time. Besides, Mother will respond better to someone other than me. I'm too close to her. She'll dig her feet in and not listen to a word I say. Another doctor will have a much better chance of getting her to do what needs to be done."

Robert hoped his theory that his mother had some form of a dementia was wrong. He hated that he had to leave the next day to get back to his practice after the family meeting. He planned to stay on top of everything that was going on with his mother. He knew Darcy and Mary would feel better knowing he would be in charge.

Darcy dried her eyes with a Kleenex. "You're like family to us, Mary," she said, standing up and holding her hands out to her mother's best friend. Robert and Mary both stood up and they all formed a circle, embracing each other.

Robert had never seen Mary and his sister look so distraught. He wanted to comfort them, but at the same time he didn't want to give them false hopes. He knew it could be a few different things. First, the doctors needed to do a thorough medical examination. He knew that if it hadn't been for Mary she could have lived in her imaginary world for too long before he and his sister found out what was going on. He prayed his mother would be okay.

They all stood quietly, thinking their own thoughts about what was happening to Clara, fearing that they were losing a mother and a best friend—and praying at the same time for a miracle.

Chapter Twenty-One

The Hospital Stay

DESPITE BEING HOOKED UP to oxygen and having her heart rhythms being monitored with wires everywhere, Clara was fidgeting with the tubing from her intravenous in anticipation of being discharged. She only wished she knew when that would be. The sun had been up for hours. She needed to get back home to her little family, especially Teddy. They must all be frantic with worry, wondering where she'd gone. She felt terrible causing a fuss, believing that nothing was wrong with her and wishing that she had never agreed to go to the hospital, and she was worried about the dolls. Although she asked Mary to check in on them, she felt that no one could take care of them the way she did.

Suddenly, a tall, stern-looking nurse appeared at Clara's door with medication in hand. She reminded

Clara of Nurse Ratched from *One Flew Over the Cuckoo's Nest*. Her coarse black hair was pulled back from her walnut-colored face into a tight little bun, and a gap showed in her front teeth.

"Hello, Mrs. ..."

"Oh, just call me Clara," she interrupted. "I'm not used to being addressed formally."

"Okay, Clara. My name is Della. I'll be your nurse for the next eight hours."

"Eight hours!" Clara yelled. "You think I am going to be here for another eight hours? You just do me a favor and call Dr. Hoyt. I have to get out of here today."

"Now, now, Clara, just hang on. Dr. Hoyt will want you to remain here until tomorrow, at least. I'm sure of that."

"No, dear, I am leaving this hospital right now," Clara suddenly announced. She flung the covers off of her and started to get out of bed, oxygen, intravenous, and monitor wires still intact.

"Hold on, Clara!" Della gently caught hold of both of Clara's shoulders and held onto her firmly to keep her from dislodging the tubing.

Finding herself short of breath, Clara had no choice but to lie back down onto the bed. It surprised her how much strength it took simply trying to get up. She could see from the look on Della's face that she'd be leaving over her nurse's dead body.

"How in the world did I get in here in the first place?" Clara grumbled. "I don't need to be in a hospital. I feel fine."

"Yes, Clara, and it is very possible the doctor will agree with you and discharge you tomorrow," Della said patiently. "He'll be in to see you sometime soon. You can talk with him then. Can you promise me you'll wait until he gets here?"

Clara closed her eyes and didn't answer.

Della soothed Clara's hand with gentle strokes. "Clara?" she whispered, lowering her head down close to Clara's ears. Clara turned to look at Della. Della repeated her question. "Will you promise me you'll wait until the doctor comes in before trying to leave?"

"Okay!" Clara shouted.

"Thank you, Clara," Della said with forced politeness. Clara turned her face away from Della so she wouldn't see the tears filling her eyes. "Is there anything you want to talk to me about, Clara?" Della asked, genuine concern filling her voice.

"No, dear. I'll be alright," Clara said with a sigh.

"Why don't you take this pill for me?"

"What is it?" Clara asked.

"It's for your heart."

"There's nothing wrong with my heart," Clara said vehemently, "and besides, I don't believe in taking drugs."

To Della's relief, Dr. Hoyt walked into the room just as Clara was making her final point. Clara turned to him and said, "Gus, I am so glad to see you. Gus, will you please tell this nice young woman that I don't need any pills."

"You need to do as your nurse says, Clara," Dr. Hoyt told her gently.

Della, now standing at the foot of Clara's bed with tray in hand, said, "She seems to be a little confused, Doctor."

"You just wait a minute, Miss whatever-your-name-is," Clara sputtered. "I am not confused."

"Clara, do you know where you are?" Dr. Hoyt asked.

"Of course, I know where I am."

"Why not tell us where you are then?" he coaxed her.

"I am at the hospital, of course." She tried to cross her arms to demonstrate her aggravation, until her intravenous reminded her of the impossibility of that mode of expression. She settled for a noisy huff.

"Which hospital are you in?" Dr. Hoyt persisted.

"What difference does it make?"

"Do you know what day it is?"

"No, and what difference does that make?"

"One last question, Clara," Dr. Hoyt asked, taking her hand in his. "Why are you in the hospital? What brought you here?"

Clara looked at Dr. Hoyt, then at Della, annoyed with all the questions that were being slung at her. One thing she did know: she didn't know the answers, and it frightened her. She began to cry. "I don't remember why I'm here. I'm confused, I guess," she added as an afterthought.

"It's okay, Clara," Dr. Hoyt said kindly. "We're here to help you."

"You came in today by ambulance with some chest pain," Della said.

"Oh. Yes. Now I remember," Clara fibbed.

Dr. Hoyt went to the opposite side of the bed and again took her hand in his. "It's going to be okay, Clara, but I want you to do as the nurse and I say so you'll get better. The sooner you get better, the sooner you can go home."

"I want to go home," Clara stated clearly, staring straight ahead of her, making eye contact with neither her doctor nor her nurse. "I have never liked being in hospitals. They give me the creeps."

"Okay, but you'll have to cooperate with the medical staff," Dr. Hoyt insisted.

"If I take the pill, can I go home tomorrow?" Clara wheedled.

"It will definitely be a step in the right direction." Dr. Hoyt smiled. Della handed Clara the pill and a cup of water. She and Clara locked eyes as Clara swallowed the pill with ease.

"That's great!" Della congratulated her.

"You make it sound like I just swam the English Channel," Clara harrumphed. Della smiled and headed for the door.

"Clara," Dr. Hoyt said carefully, "this isn't the first time you've been in the hospital, you know. You were here a few weeks ago."

"Oh, yes. I remember now." She did have a vague recollection, but the details escaped her. "Did I have to stay in the hospital that time?"

"No, Clara, you were released the same night. That's why I wanted you to stay this time, so I can really do a thorough work-up on you."

"Well, that's good. Why didn't you just tell me that in the first place? Think I can go home tomorrow, Gus?"

"I don't know, Clara. We'll see. There's a family meeting tomorrow," he added.

Clara got her back up again. "What do we need to have that for?"

Dr. Hoyt could see he'd pushed a button. Clara asked him if he knew about her new friends, and if he would ask Mary if she would bring them with her to the hospital when she visited later on. Dr. Hoyt smiled affectionately at her and agreed. He didn't want to do anything to upset her. He could see clearly that these new friends meant a lot to her.

Chapter Twenty-Two

A Moonlight Ride
in Old Faithful

R OBERT NORMALLY ENJOYED SLEEPING in his bedroom. Clara hadn't changed a thing since he had left for college. Tonight, however, he couldn't sleep; his mother was on his mind. He tried counting sheep, then counting to a hundred, then finally gave up and decided to read, but he couldn't concentrate.

He was thankful Mary was such a big help to the family, and he loved her for it. He smiled, recalling the time she'd agreed to go for a ride one afternoon on *Old Faithful*, Robert's well-used rowboat. He'd finally get a chance to impress Mary with his boating skills. And Darcy had come along for the ride.

∞

The temperature was holding steady at seventy-eight degrees, with a warm zephyr breeze. The sound of a few seagulls filled the air. Other than an occasional sound of a motorboat off in the distance, they had the lake to themselves. The oars glided through the water in rhythmic motion as they rowed across the lake, the dark-green water gently lapping at the sides of the boat. Darcy was on one green oar; Robert was on the other.

Hundreds of thick elms and evergreens surrounded the lake. No one spoke. They were all mesmerized by the peaceful beauty of nature.

Mary sat in the middle of the boat with a smile on her face and her hands folded in her lap. Her straw hat with a wide red ribbon was tilted over her eyes, protecting them from the afternoon sun. It matched her red and white summer dress. It meant so much to Robert for Mary to come out and witness his boating skills. It was impossible to get his mother or father to ever come out on the lake with him. Clara couldn't swim—she was afraid of water—and Frank wouldn't take the time away from work.

After an hour of rowing, Darcy had gotten tired and stopped. Robert wanted to row over to a small, deserted island, one of his favorite places to visit when he was out on the lake. He wanted to show it to Mary.

When they reached the island, they were all happy to rest. The three of them all relaxed for a while, stretched out on the sand, listening to the water brush over the rocks. It was so peaceful. Through the thick forest on the island, they listened to the sound of birds and the gentle wind brushing through the trees. "This is heaven," Mary said. Robert was happy she was enjoying his special place.

Then they headed back. Oars in hand, they began to row in the direction of home, but Darcy refused to row. She was being stubborn, and started to whimper that she was hungry and tired. Mary tried to help, but she couldn't get the hang of it.

It didn't take long for them to figure out that while they were relaxing on the island, the current changed, making it impossible to make any headway. Robert was rowing against the breeze. The more he rowed, the further back they went, heading away from the shore and home.

Robert was becoming exhausted and finally had to admit to them that he couldn't row anymore—that they would just have to hope and pray that the current would shift directions. He put his oars down and rested his head against the bow of the boat. He didn't want them to know that he was scared and tired, or that the clouds were building by the minute.

To their dismay, the current continued to push them even further up the lake, far from either shore. Darcy put her head down and rested it on her knees. Her whole body was shaking and she began to cry.

Mary got up in the middle of the boat, causing it to sway from side to side as she made her way down to the other end where Darcy was sitting. She put her arms around her shoulders, patted her back, and said, "We'll be okay, honey." She told her the current would shift in a while; they'd just have to wait it out.

"But it's getting dark," Darcy wailed. "How will we find our way back home?"

"Robert knows where we're headed and how to get back." But Robert wasn't sure how far the wind had pushed them or where they were. Even worse, he could sense a storm was brewing.

Mary was trying hard to be brave. Then she told Robert something that he would never forget. She reassured him that he would get them all back safely, that he was a smart young man whom she trusted with her life. It was a huge confidence boost for Robert; no one had ever put that much faith in him. He always wished that his dad would make him feel that way.

The sun suddenly broke through the clouds close to the horizon; there was only about half an hour before dark. If the current didn't change in the next half hour, they'd be stuck on the lake for the night— maybe in the middle of a terrible storm.

"Maybe we should start praying," Robert suggested.

"Stop it, Robert," Darcy said, crying even harder. "You're scaring us. It's entirely your fault for taking us to that stupid island. We don't even have anything to bail out the water if it starts raining." Then, through her sniffling and sobbing, she said, "I don't want to die."

"Now stop it, Darcy," Mary said. "We are not going to die."

Mary asked Robert to pray first, but he declined and asked Mary to do so instead. He had heard her preach on Sunday and knew she could get God's attention.

Before she started, she asked Robert and Mary to close their eyes and not to look up until she was finished. "Now, Lord," she began, "I know you don't want anything to happen to us out here. I know you hear all prayers, even from people who don't know you, Lord. I know you can make miracles happen, and Lord, we sure need one now. Please get us all safely back to shore and home, Father. I ask this in your precious son Jesus's name. Amen. Oh, and one more thing, Lord. When we get back, I pray their mother won't take a stick to their butts."

With that, she smiled and looked up at Darcy, who was just opening her eyes. But Robert couldn't smile. He was hoping Mary was right, and that their dad wouldn't find out. He knew he was in trouble if he did. His dad had forbidden him to go over to the island.

At dusk, Mary's prayer was answered. The current suddenly changed direction and the wind picked up simultaneously, pushing them in the right direction. Off in the distance they could see a light from somebody's house, and Robert rowed them to it, with the help of the wind. Robert believed to this day it was a miracle.

When they landed at the dock, they found themselves face to face with a policeman. The officer questioned Mary about what happened and was satisfied with her answers. Robert knew that if Mary hadn't been there, he'd have been in trouble.

He could still remember the policeman radioing headquarters. "It's okay. Just a few moonlight riders outracing the storm." He made it sound like it was just another night. But it wasn't, not for them.

God answered Robert's prayer that night, because Mary never told his parents about their moonlight ride in *Old Faithful* back from the island.

Robert glanced over at the clock. It was 1:00 a.m. He closed his eyes and tried again to drift off to sleep, wishing he could stop the wheels from turning in his head.

The family meeting was going to be stressful. Something had to be done for his mother. One thing was clear: she couldn't live alone.

Robert finally fell off to sleep, still thinking about the family meeting the next day, hoping for the best for his mother. As he pictured her sleeping with the dolls and the teddy bear lying beside her, he fought back the tears that were on the verge of streaming down his cheeks.

Chapter Twenty-Three

The Family Meeting

T HE MEETING STARTED ON time. Seated at a round table in the hospital conference room were both Dr. Hoyt and the geriatric psychologist, Dr. Cook; the social worker, Miss Young; Clara's nurse, Della; and Mary, Robert, and Darcy. They had decided to have Clara join them later on in the meeting.

Dr. Hoyt spoke first. "Let's all start by introducing ourselves." Each one did as instructed, then Dr. Hoyt began.

"I have known Clara for many years," he said. "Her family has been under my care since I started practicing in South Port. Thanks for coming, Darcy. Robert, jump in any time. We welcome your professional knowledge." Both smiled and nodded their appreciation to Dr. Hoyt.

Turning to face Mary, he said, "and you, my dear, have been my client for many years as well." Mary smiled. "Thanks for coming. "I am sorry that we have to be here for such an unhappy reason. Clara is a fine person. Our goal here is to do our best to find out what is causing the problems with her heart and to rule out any possibility of dementia. I will be speaking about her heart condition, and then I will let Dr. Cook share his findings. He met with Clara this morning."

Dr. Hoyt put on his reading glasses, picked up Clara's chart, and flipped through it until he found the page he wanted. "I have done extensive blood work and have just gotten the results back. I found significant abnormalities in several areas." Consulting the page in her chart, he ran a finger down until he reached the first problem number. "The most disturbing are her hemoglobin, which is low, and others that have to do with what she is eating—or not eating." He stopped to clear his throat, then returned to the report and continued speaking in his confident voice.

He went on to say her electrolytes were off and her potassium was a little low, while her sodium was high. An echocardiogram was done as well as some other tests he felt were necessary. He found some abnormalities there as well. The results were clear that she had angina, he added, and although the EKG showed some deterioration in the walls of the heart, he felt it was unnecessary to treat at this time. It was all part of the aging process, he felt.

He stated the importance of treating her high blood pressure and getting it under control to cut down on the angina attacks. Given her age, he would prefer not to be too aggressive, but he wanted to prevent her from having a cerebral vascular attack, better known as a stroke. Dr. Hoyt explained that when Clara was not taking her medication properly, it contributed to the problem, including her confusion.

Darcy rolled her eyes. "What on earth was Mother thinking?" she wondered aloud. Dr Hoyt chose to take her question as rhetorical, and continued.

He told the family he would treat Clara with appropriate medication and that he would monitor her heart condition regularly.

He explained he would start her back on medication for the angina. Since there were a number of different blood pressure medications on the market, some of which he liked and others that he felt wouldn't be a good choice for Clara, he wanted to think about it, and would let everyone know as soon as he decided. The problem with a certain heart medication, he continued, was that someone would need to take her pulse before she gets it every day. Clara was obviously not going to be able to do it herself.

"I'll let Dr. Cook share his findings with us and then we'll go from there. Dr. Cook?"

Dr. Cook, a tall, thin, blonde young man, began. He introduced himself to the family and added how impressed he was to see all of her family present and Mary as well. "From the medical record and my exam of Clara this morning, I am not convinced Clara has dementia." There was a general sigh of relief from Darcy, Robert, and Mary.

"Then what do you think is causing her confusion, the hallucinating, the talking to the dolls and all that?" Mary asked before Robert or Darcy could voice the same question.

"Obviously her rather deep loneliness and sense of loss are a part of the picture," Dr. Cook began. "Yet I primarily think it could be delirium, caused by her electrolyte imbalances and other matters related to poor nutrition, and of course taking her medication improperly," Dr. Cook suggested.

He told them it was a mental disturbance, of relatively short duration, usually reflecting a toxic state.

"It appears she hasn't been eating right for a period of time," he added.

"That's just it," Mary said with a shake of her head, "She says she doesn't like to eat. I've been around her enough to know that when she does eat, she doesn't eat well. She eats a lot of those frozen dinners because it's easy for her and a lot of sandwiches, and way too many sweets, in my opinion. She'll make a sandwich and call it a meal. I've tried to talk to her about eating healthy, but she's pretty stubborn."

"Yes, I've noticed," chuckled Dr. Cook. Robert and Darcy smiled, acknowledging that trying to get Clara to do something she didn't want to could be virtually impossible.

"She could be forgetting to eat because of all her confusion lately," Mary suggested.

"That's probably correct," Dr. Cook agreed. "We need to rule out dementia, but before we can do that, we need to get her medically stabilized. And to do that, she needs to start eating right and taking in lots of fluids. Dehydration is also a problem. The forgetfulness could be just a part of the normal aging process. But complicated by poor eating habits, it can only get worse. However, I want you to remember that confusion and hallucinations can go along with delirium. What I don't want is for all of us to jump to any conclusions right away. Personally, I'd like to see Clara in a situation where she's not living alone, not for a while anyway, while everything can be monitored and she can socialize more."

Miss Young, the social worker, spoke next, addressing Mary, Darcy, and Robert primarily. "I met with Clara, both yesterday and today. I gathered information from all of you, as well as from Clara."

She got right to the point and said her vote was that Clara go to a facility, at least temporarily. Then she asked if anyone from the family had anything they would like to say.

Robert spoke up and said he didn't want his mother going into a nursing home any more than she did. On the other hand, he knew his mother had been lonelier than he'd realized. He knew the socialization she would get from being in a nursing home or an assisted-living situation would give her contact with other people. He knew her relationship with the dolls was, in part, because she felt so lonely. He also knew Darcy and Mary both felt the same. Obviously, something had to be done, but nothing seemed to be a proper fit. He felt torn by conflicting emotions, like one grasping at straws, and none of the options discussed would not pang his conscience were he to assent to it.

"Isolation in the elderly can oftentimes cause confusion and hallucinations of different kinds, correct?" Robert asked Dr. Cook. The doctor nodded.

"Hallucinations or delusions ranging from voices to some pretty unusual behaviors are possible, and I believe that in Clara's case, first not taking her medication as prescribed, then her increased isolation, may have triggered the confusion. That, added to her poor eating habits, in turn set a delirium in motion. Kind of like the domino effect, or like a snowball rolling down a hill that grows bigger and bigger the farther it goes." He stopped and looked around the table, and asked if it all made sense to everyone.

Robert, Darcy, and Mary all nodded in unison. The social worker said she felt Clara needed to be in some form of supervised setting for the short term, at least until she was medically stable and capable of caring for herself again. She asked if anyone had a solution other than a short-term nursing home or assisted-living stay.

Silence filled the room. Thoughts hung heavy in the air like smoke from a cigar. No one spoke until Robert finally broke the silence. He offered to try to get his mother to come and stay with him and his family, but he knew her. The chances of that would be slim to none.

Darcy told the group rather coolly that there was no way she could take the time from work. She wondered whether someone could stay with Clara.

Miss Young pointed out that it would be costly to hire around-the-clock nursing care, but felt it would work.

Mary interjected. "I may be able to convince her to stay with me, at least for a while, until she can get back to her old self again."

Robert smiled and thanked Mary, but felt she was being way too generous. But Mary insisted. "I can't bear the thought of her going to a nursing home."

Everyone in the room agreed that if Clara could stay with Mary, it would solve the immediate problem.

The social worker left the room and went to get Clara; it was time to bring her into the loop. Robert, Darcy, and Mary sat in silent prayer, hoping for a miracle. As they waited, Robert couldn't help but think back to that day on the lake. *Mary truly is a good soul. What would the family do without her always being there in a time of need?*

Miss Young wheeled Clara into the conference room, her dolls and Teddy neatly arranged in their basket on her lap. Her eyes lit up at the sight of her two children and Mary.

The social worker situated Clara at the table in between Darcy and Robert. In turn, she kissed each of them on the cheek, then blew a kiss to Mary, who was sitting across from Robert. "Hello, Mary," she said with a little wave. "I didn't know you would be here too."

Mary didn't let on that she'd told Clara the day before that she would see her at the family meeting.

It was just one more thing that Clara had forgotten. "Hello, Clara dear," Mary said from where she sat. "How are you feeling today?"

"I feel just fine. I want to go home today," Clara said firmly, then raised her head defiantly and set her jaw.

Dr. Hoyt had agreed to be the bad guy and lay down the law to Clara about her having to stay with Mary.

If he gave her no alternative, she'd have no reason to be angry with either her children or with Mary. Those three had to remain on good terms with her.

Dr. Hoyt got right to the point. "I guess I've got some good news and some bad news for you, Clara. The tests came back showing you have some angina, which we need to give you medicine for every day. This medication requires that somebody be able to take your pulse before you receive it. And you are going to need to take another pill for elevated blood pressure. I am recommending you not go back home, temporarily, while you're monitored twenty-four seven. Later—let's say in another two or three weeks—we will reevaluate you for going back home. That's the bad news." Clara clearly agreed.

"Now, the good news," he said and paused. "The good news, Clara, is that Mary has offered for you to stay with her."

Clara sat motionless, looking around the table at all the eyes that were focused on her. The room was quiet. Everyone was holding their breath for her reaction, bracing themselves for a fight.

Clara finally responded. "Mary, can my little family come too? You know Teddy especially hates to be alone. He banged the loudest to get out of the box he was in."

Mary got up from her seat and walked over to kiss Clara on the cheek. "Of course," she said.

Chapter Twenty-Four

An Affair Revealed

THAT AFTERNOON ROBERT SAID his goodbyes and headed back home; he had to get back to work. He could see that Clara's thinking was already starting to clear. It made leaving that much easier. It felt right leaving his mother with Mary. He knew it was what she wanted.

Clara's pleading eyes longed for Darcy to stay longer, but Darcy had to head back home as well. She had so much to do at work, she told her mother; she knew Mary could handle all the details for a smooth discharge.

"The fact is," Darcy admitted to Mary privately, "I wouldn't have a clue how to handle Mother's care." She knew Mary used to be a nurse, and could certainly take her pulse. She also knew, as Robert did, that Mary knew how to take a blood pressure, if it came to that. Mother couldn't be in better hands.

Mary smiled, deciding to just go along with the plan even though she knew the real reason Darcy was leaving. Clara didn't have to know Darcy had a choice. She could take a leave of absence from her job and stay and help her mother. Or she could take the bonus that was being offered to her if she returned to her job a day early.

Mary knew that although Darcy loved her mother, she also loved her work. She secretly wondered if there was some other reason why Darcy wanted to leave. *It will all come out in the wash,* she mused. *It wouldn't surprise me if Darcy had something up her sleeve.*

"Are you sure it's okay for me to leave tomorrow, Mary?" Darcy asked, interrupting her train of thought. "I'll stay if you need me to." But Mary knew Darcy was itching to go home, and that she was holding her breath hoping that she would say she didn't need her help.

"You have a safe trip home, honey," Mary said. "We'll be fine. Clara's already forgotten you have to leave in the morning. Forgetfulness has its rewards," she added with a smile as she hugged the young woman tenderly. Darcy couldn't help being Darcy.

∞

Darcy and Mary left the hospital together and drove back to Clara's house, Darcy happy that her mother would have such good care with Mary at the helm. Mary had already begun taking charge of the situation. The visiting nurse would be coming first thing in the morning.

When Darcy went downstairs to the kitchen, she found Mary making tea for both of them. Standing in the doorway, she watched Mary, who stood tall with her head held high, as if she were balancing a stack of books atop it. She was wearing a pair of black slacks and a red long-sleeve turtleneck.

Mary was humming a song Darcy had heard her sing many times before. She smiled, recalling how happy Mary could be, even in the midst of trouble. She was a strong woman, capable of making the best of a difficult situation. "Take charge" was written all over her, a pillar of salt.

Darcy cleared her throat in an effort to get her attention, but Mary was so caught up in her humming, she didn't hear her. Darcy tried clearing her throat again but still Mary didn't hear. Finally, Darcy had no choice but to walk up behind her and tap her on the shoulder, to which Mary jumped in surprise.

"I'm sorry to have startled you. I tried to get your attention, but your focus was on the song. What's the name of the song you're humming?"

Mary told her it was an old gospel hymn called "Somebody Prayed for Me" that she sang for many years in the choir. "Until I got mad at that old church," Mary laughed. "People always fussing and fighting over everything." She told Darcy that one day she just stopped going. Her mother used to tell her that you can still get to heaven if you're a Christian, even if you don't go to church. She also said there are more devils and sinners in the church than out. They both laughed.

Mary took a mug from the shelf. It read, "Love Makes the World Go Round." She dropped a tea bag in it and poured in the hot water, then handed it to Darcy, who stared at the words on the mug she'd just been given. Mary could tell she had something on her mind.

Then she reached back up into the cupboard for a mug for herself. The one she chose this time read, "Miracles Come from God."

"I like yours better, Mary," Darcy said quietly. "It's a miracle Mother is going to be okay and another miracle that we have you in this family."

The two women sat down at the kitchen table and drank their tea. As she ran her finger around her cup, Darcy was uncharacteristically quiet. "Drink your tea, dear," Mary said. "Before it gets cold." Darcy took a sip and put the mug down, but still didn't speak. "What is it, Darcy?" Mary said, concerned. "You look so sad."

Darcy sighed. "Mary," she said finally, looking the older woman in the eyes, "I know I can trust you to keep a secret."

Mary set her mug on the table and placed her strong, warm hand on Darcy's shoulder. "What's the matter, honey?"

"Mother would never approve," Darcy began, "but I hope you'll understand." Mary suddenly got the sense that a bomb was about to explode.

"What it all boils down to is ... I'm dating a married man," Darcy blurted out.

"A married man! What in the world's gotten into you?" Mary couldn't hold back the words or her astonishment.

"I love him," Darcy said plaintively. "We tried not to fall in love. It just happened. He's so perfect for me, except, of course, that he's married."

Dumbfounded, Mary sat staring at Darcy as the younger woman unraveled a heartfelt, tangled love story of how she and her married man had met, an affair that involved not two but three lives. *Why should I be surprised, though?* she thought. *Darcy never did anything simple.* Mary finally shook her head and sighed. *Well, Darcy's gone and gotten herself into a fine mess this time,* she thought. *If she thinks any good could ever come from it, she's sadly mistaken.*

Mary knew Darcy needed to unload what she was going through on someone, and she and Darcy had always been able to confide in one another. Something like this she never could tell her mother, even if she were well. Mary could tell when she finished talking, she was glad she got it out in the open. Darcy knew her secret was safe with her. Mary didn't like keeping it from Clara, but this was something Mary knew Clara couldn't handle, at least not now.

The sun started its descent down through the big oak tree that stood in the backyard just as clouds began to pile in. A monumental rainstorm, predicted for later that night, was on its way. Darcy glanced out the window and jumped up from the table. She didn't want to get caught in the storm. She had to get her rental car back to the airport so she needed extra time. They gave each other a warm hug, and Darcy got her things together and was on her way.

Three hours later, Darcy sat on a plane heading home, wishing she had never told Mary. She could kick herself now, though she felt certain Mary could handle it. However, judging by how much the news had shocked her, Darcy was glad her mother didn't know about her married lover.

Chapter Twenty-Five

The Love Letter

ONCE DARCY WAS GONE, Mary decided to get a few of Clara's clothes together. She hoped to find Clara's Medicare card as well. Darcy said she didn't have time to find it, and asked Mary if she wouldn't mind. She headed for Clara's bedroom, still in shock over what Darcy had told her.

Clara's bureau drawers contained a large, neat assortment of blouses and various other pieces of clothing. Mary was reaching in and about to pull out a blouse when her hand encountered a box underneath the blouse.

Moving the blouse to one side, she saw a box covered with a tapestry design of browns and gold, about half the size of a shoebox. Stopping to ponder it for a few moments, she wondered if she should open it or not, then decided that she would. How else was she to find Clara's Medicare card?

Expecting knickknacks of some sort, Mary was surprised to find that the box contained a letter. She opened the letter, which started, "Dear Clara, please forgive me but I had to ..."

Mary's eyes skipped down to the signature at the bottom. It was signed, "All my love, Dave."

Standing motionless with the letter in hand, Mary put her hand up to her mouth to stifle the sound coming from her. Briskly shaking her head side to side, as if trying to bring some sort of clarity to her thinking, she quickly calculated the years and realized it would mean that the letter was written before Clara and Frank had been married.

Mary knew Dave, Frank's best man at the wedding. How could she forget? She'd been the maid of honor. Dave and Frank had been friends for years, but Dave disappeared after the wedding and never resurfaced. Frank had mentioned Dave once or twice and even tried to find him at one point, but had finally given up. It had always seemed odd to Mary that Dave would disappear like that, without a trace. No one seemed to know what had become of him. They'd always feared the worst.

Mary started to read more, then felt guilty. She couldn't go invading Clara's privacy. It wouldn't be right. She felt ashamed of herself for even considering such a thing.

Folding the letter neatly, she placed it back in the box and put the box back in the drawer. Then she began gathering a few pieces of clothing she knew Clara would need. She was curious about the letter, but swore she'd never mention it to Clara. If Clara wanted her to know about Dave, she'd tell her. Any thoughts Mary had about Clara and Dave would be kept locked up in her memory. Clara's secrets were safe with her.

But Mary woke the next day with the thought of the letter she'd found on her mind. She couldn't help but wonder what happened between Clara and Dave, and why Clara had a secret that she never shared with her. They never kept anything from one another. They were best friends. Mary wondered if she should ask Clara about it someday, when the time was right. But she dropped the subject, knowing that the most important thing right now was Clara getting better.

Then she thought of Darcy and the mess she had gotten herself into. *There are way too many secrets floating around!* Mary thought. *And I'm more involved than I want to be in this situation of Darcy's, that's for sure.*

Mary sat at her kitchen table making a list of everything she needed to do in preparation for Clara's stay. For now, she needed to concentrate on Clara. Darcy would have to wait.

She was excited about being able to help Clara. It was the least she could do. She decided to make up a menu for the week. It would be fun to get Clara involved in planning the meals. Clara's secret had already begun to fade into the back of Mary's mind. Mary was clear on one thing, though: in no uncertain terms should Clara know anything about Darcy's love triangle. For now, Mary needed to focus on all that would be necessary to get Clara on her feet again, and good meals were a good place to start. Mary couldn't wait to tackle the challenge of putting some meat on Clara's bones with some of her good home cooking.

Mary found herself wondering if Clara would be carrying the dolls and stuffed bear around with her all day like she'd been doing before she went into the hospital. She felt certain that if she and Clara could get busy doing something interesting and fun, maybe she wouldn't need the dolls.

Mary went deep into thought on the subject, and as she often did on troubling subjects, she decided to pray. It always made her feel good to give a problem to the Lord. She had no doubt He could handle any situation. She bowed her head.

"Dear heavenly Father, I am calling on you this morning, not for me, but for Clara. Lord, she needs you to help her to get well. Yes, Lord, your child is in need of help. How can I help her, Lord? Heavenly Father, make it plain what I can do. I was thinking that if we could just get involved in doing something, Lord, she might put away those dolls and be her old self again. I'll be looking for the answer, Lord. And, Lord, one more thing: please let Clara know that she can tell me anything she wants to, even a long-kept secret ... in Jesus's name, Amen."

Mary was wise enough to know that we get what we need, not always what we want, in this life, and that the Lord is always right on time.

Mary called the hospital social worker to finalize the discharge plan, wanting to be sure that everything was in order. Miss Young assured her that plans for Clara's release were under control and on schedule.

Clara's stubborn, but she is also a tough ol' girl, Mary thought. She knew her friend had the spunk and spirit to get better.

She took a big vitamin book off the shelf and dusted the cover with a Kleenex she fished from the pocket of her bathrobe. Then she picked up her glasses from the table and put them on. Her long, aged fingers carefully turned the pages of the book until she came to the index. Scrolling down the page, she finally came to "Angina." She turned to page eighty-eight.

The paragraph on angina suggested several supplements. Once she finished reading everything she could that pertained to Clara's condition, she closed the book, satisfied with what she needed to buy.

It didn't surprise her that not one of the doctors had talked about supplements. Mary knew how important they are. She would make sure Clara took them daily. She knew Clara took a multivitamin every day, but she also knew she needed more than just that. She glanced down her list, and then put it in her pocketbook. She felt certain Doctor Hoyt would okay them.

She could just picture Clara and herself this summer, working in the garden. She could easily imagine Clara, shovel in hand, in her dirt-stained coveralls, planting geraniums, pansies, and marigolds as her wide-brimmed straw hat kept the hot sun out of her eyes.

People often stopped to admire both their gardens every summer. Working the garden together had become a tradition of Clara and Mary's. They had fun trying to see who could grow the biggest flowers. It was always a tie. Mary knew it would be good for Clara to be active again, and she couldn't wait to see her smiling face.

The clock was ticking. She still had shopping to do and vitamins to buy at the health food store before she went to pick Clara up from the hospital.

Meanwhile, at the hospital, Clara was sitting up in bed, draining the last drop of her coffee. She stared down at her untouched eggs and toast. She just couldn't eat. She was too excited about leaving. Even though she wasn't going to her home, she was glad enough to be getting out of the hospital.

She moved the bedside table to one side so she could get a better look at the dolls and Teddy. Sarah, Frances, Baby, and Teddy were lined up at the foot of her bed, their eyes fixed in her direction, their predictable, painted-on smiles frozen in place. They seemed as real to her as any family could be, and they made her smile.

"Did you know that we're leaving the hospital today?" she asked them. "We'll be staying with Mary for a few days. I know you'll enjoy Mary. She's my best friend, you know."

Chapter Twenty-Six

Settling In

URING THE DRIVE HOME, Mary glanced over at Clara. She couldn't help but smile at how happy Clara looked, with the dolls and Teddy wrapped neatly in their basket on her lap.

Mary's silver Chevrolet pulled into her driveway. Clara had clambered out of the car as soon as Mary turned off the engine. As the two of them stood in the driveway, Mary saw Clara gaze wistfully over at her own little white house.

"Mary," Clara asked quietly, "do you think it would be okay if I went home, just to check on things? I won't stay long. I just want to get my friends some new clothes."

Mary had suspected Clara might want to go home. She knew it wouldn't be a good idea. She also felt that once Clara got inside her home she wouldn't want to leave. Mary had promised Robert and Darcy she would do everything she could to keep Clara busy so she wouldn't have time to miss her home.

What Mary hadn't anticipated was Clara wanting to get the dolls new outfits. Momentarily speechless, she knew she didn't want to upset Clara by saying no. On the other hand, if she didn't set a few hard rules, Clara might want to go home and stay permanently.

Mary finally blurted out the words that were stuck like a cotton ball in her throat. She told her it would be better to get inside where it was warm, and she should get settled in and have some lunch. She had a feeling Clara wasn't eating well in the hospital and wanted to prepare a hearty meal for her.

"Lunch sounds good; I'm hungry." Clara turned and headed for Mary's place. Mary breathed a sigh of relief, but she knew it was going to be difficult for Clara to let go of the idea of wanting to be in her own home. She had her work cut her for her; she knew Clara could be stubborn. She knew Clara loved her home with all her heart. But she also knew Clara was strong and, with time, would settle into the temporary situation with her if she could just keep her occupied. Mary brought everything she thought Clara needed and had it neatly organized upstairs in Clara's room. What she hadn't thought of were the dolls' clothes. She would find a way to sneak back over to Clara's later in the day and get them. She hoped Clara would take a nap, making it easier for Mary to slip away unnoticed.

The two women sat at the kitchen table eating meatloaf, Harvard beets, and mashed potatoes with gravy. The dolls sat at the table in their basket next to Clara. Mary was thrilled to see her eat a decent meal, and even more thrilled to see how happy Clara was.

They talked and laughed nonstop about the old days, each one recalling old stories of the past. Afterwards, they got busy making a cake from one of Mary's favorite recipes, and then they spent a quiet afternoon knitting.

The day flew by. Much to Mary's relief, Clara didn't repeat her request to go home. She had been silently rehearsing what she would say if Clara did ask.

Mary was surprised at how tired Clara was. She fell asleep on the couch after dinner, the dolls and Teddy by her side. Mary took the opportunity to slip across the yard to Clara's and grab the dolls' clothes.

When they went upstairs to bed the first night, Clara called across the hall to Mary. Mary leaped out of bed to the guest room, worried that something was wrong. "Did you want something, dear?" she asked from the doorway.

"Yes," Clara said forlornly, "I wondered if you could get the dolls and Teddy for me. I forgot them. They're still downstairs."

Mary couldn't help but smile to herself. Clara's first day had been a success. She ate most of her meals and seemed content being with her. She hadn't brought up going to her house again; she had even forgotten to take the dolls and Teddy with her when she went upstairs to bed. It was Mary's hope and prayer she would forget about them altogether, and replace them with real people. Mary planned to try to convince her once again to join the senior center in South Port, which was going to take some doing.

The next day was just as successful as the day before. Mary knew Clara was going to get better. She'd been pleased with Robert and Darcy's reactions to how much better Clara seemed to them when they'd talked to her on the phone.

"You know, Clara," Mary said as they sat in the living room having tea just before bed one day, "it just doesn't make sense that people should live alone, unless, of course, they want to. I'd forgotten how good it feels to have someone living in this house besides myself. These old walls have enjoyed the sounds of laughter. Houses were made to be lived in. I think I like the idea of not being alone." She smiled wistfully, gazing into the crackling fire.

It felt strange to Mary to be having a conversation with Clara about how much she was enjoying having someone in her home. She had never imagined how comforting it could feel. She guessed some things should be changed as one aged. She knew some ideas do change and become things of the past as people adopt new outlooks on life. Adapting to getting old should be smooth, not rough and bumpy like a ride down an old dirt road. She chuckled at the image.

She reminded Clara about how they had the same birthday, which was coming up next month, and asked her if she would like to have a real birthday party and invite her family. Clara loved the idea. They both agreed that they should do something special besides just eating a home-cooked meal as they usually did each year.

"You know, Clara," she continued, "you're welcome to stay here as long as you want. I'm enjoying having the company. I hope you like it here enough to stay with me longer than planned, but of course it will have to be your decision. I wouldn't want to force anything on you, dear."

When Clara didn't answer, Mary turned to find her sound asleep on the couch. She looked peaceful. Mary glanced across the room. The dolls and Teddy smiled back at her from the couch next to Clara.

Chapter Twenty-Seven

A Friendship Blossoms

THE DAYS TURNED INTO weeks. Clara and Mary were enjoying each other's company. Clara was reluctant at first, but then later agreed to go to the senior center two days a week. To her surprise, she liked going more than she ever imagined she would, mainly due to the fact that she almost immediately made a new friend, Florence. Mary was happy Clara was going to the center. She'd put off going to the center herself, and had stopped volunteering because she didn't want to leave Clara. Eventually, she hoped she could get back to what she enjoyed.

Florence Foster, Clara's new friend, wore thick, brown-rimmed glasses and kept her dyed red hair short. She was short, round, and jolly. Both Clara and Mary enjoyed her sense of humor and no-nonsense attitude. She moved about on a cane, when she could remember where she'd last put it.

Clara and Florence sat together talking endlessly, though at times neither of them could recall any of their conversation even a minute after it had been said. Clara rambled on and on about Darcy and of course Robert, his wife, Jean, and her grandchildren, Bret and Sara. Florence typically bragged about her son, Paul.

The couch in the community room quickly became their usual spot. They enjoyed listening to the soothing tunes that filled the warm and cheerful room. "Let Me Call You Sweetheart" was one of Clara's favorites. Floor-to-ceiling windows made the room bright and illuminated the enormously popular elderly daycare center.

While Clara and Florence talked and laughed endlessly, their time at the center sped by. They both liked Nellie, the activity helper who often played the piano. Mealtime and bingo were two of the other activities that couldn't keep them apart, although chair yoga was not a favorite.

Florence was a widow too. Both of them comforted one another about having to spend the rest of their lives without husbands. Florence finally stopped pushing Paul to move back to South Port. After enough arguments, Florence had decided to let sleeping dogs lie. Whenever the subject came up, he insisted it would make more sense for her to move to Florida and live near him. He was making more money than he could ever make in South Port.

Clara agreed to leave the dolls and Teddy at Mary's while she spent time at the center. To everyone's delight, she was growing less and less interested in the dolls. Mary knew it wouldn't be long before Clara would forget about the dolls. She was still forgetful, but the banging was gone for good. Her suspicion and the doctor's had been right, once Clara had companionship, the noises became a thing of the past.

Clara's living with Mary was the icing on the cake. Robert and Darcy, too, were happy their mother wasn't living alone, at least for now. Clearly, she did better living with someone else. They thought that eventually Mary would want her own living space back to herself, but for now, their mother was in the best possible place.

Robert was sitting in his office at the hospital. It was the end of a busy day and he was gathering his thoughts before leaving to go home. His mother had been on his mind off and on throughout the day. He was trying to decide if he should pay her a visit this weekend or the following. He hadn't been to see her since she left the hospital and he found himself missing her more than usual. He called her regularly, but he was feeling the need to be in her presence at least for a few days so he could see firsthand how his mother was getting along.

Mary told Robert that Clara no longer obsessed over the dolls. His mother was active again, almost back to her old self. She had been going to the senior center, and found a new friend. Mary was happy for her, as were Robert and Darcy. As a psychologist, Robert had plenty of first-hand experience with the phenomenon of people often replacing human contact with imaginary objects or some other unhealthy thing or situation, especially when they experienced deep isolation.

Robert knew he and Darcy had Mary to thank for his mother's remarkable gains. He wanted to think of some way to repay her. He'd offered her money more than once, but she had adamantly refused to take any. She felt that she was part of the family; she shouldn't be paid for doing what families normally do for someone they love, she'd told him. "So let that be enough about that," she'd said, putting the subject to rest.

As Robert tidied the top of his desk, he decided to call his mother. He wanted to see her. He knew her birthday was coming up.

When he got there, he planned to talk with Mary about Clara making the transition back to her own home. As much as he hated to admit it, time was up. It was time that Mary had her house to herself again. The one thing he and Darcy did not want to do was to take advantage of a good situation. Even so, he wasn't looking forward to it. He wished Clara could stay with Mary indefinitely.

The phone rang just as Clara was setting the table for dinner. She enjoyed having tasks to do around Mary's house; setting the table and cleaning up after the meal was her designated job. Mary preferred cooking to cleaning any day.

Clara answered the phone. Happy to hear Robert's voice, she started telling him about her day at the center, then stopped herself when she realized she was rambling on about herself.

"I'm coming tomorrow for the weekend," Robert told her. Clara was overjoyed, and called to Mary to tell her the good news.

"That's wonderful," Mary said. "Tell him that he is welcome to join in on our birthday party and stay here if he wants to. I have plenty of room."

Clara turned back to the phone. "Robert, did you hear Mary?"

"Tell her I'd be glad to stay," Robert said. "I don't want to miss out on her home cooking and the birthday party."

Clara settled back into her conversation with Robert, telling him all about Florence. She told him she was amazed that she and Florence had never met until now and they both had lived in South Port all their lives. She also told him that she wasn't sitting around thinking about nothing. She told him that Mary kept her pretty busy helping around her big house, and how pleased Mary was with her helping. She told him she was doing her share and not just sitting around taking up space. She felt it was the least she could do, and she enjoyed it.

Robert hung up the phone. He was glad he was going to visit his mother, but was not looking forward to telling her that it was time for her to go back home. *She is doing so well,* he thought. *She's enjoying herself for a change.* Robert sat back in his chair, took in a deep breath, and let it out slowly.

He closed his eyes. He'd had a busy week and was looking forward to going home to relax in front of the television with a cold beer. Then he found himself wondering if Jean and the kids might like to take a drive with him for the weekend. There certainly was enough room at Mary's. He would ask.

Locking his desk file cabinet, he turned off the lights and went home.

Chapter Twenty-Eight

A Family Decision

O N THE DRIVE HOME, Robert was debating the best approach to give his mom the news that she had to go back home. He thought of a few different scenarios. He could remind her that she had a lot of unfinished business in the house, like disposing of Frank's old clothes and cleaning out all of his tools from the basement. He would help her. Or he could just tell her the truth—Mary's hospitality had to come to an end, to put it bluntly. It just wasn't right to impose on her any longer. He knew how to say the words with kindness, so as not to make his mother feel that she had thoughtlessly overstayed her visit.

To the contrary, clearly the two women had been enjoying each other, but Robert felt he had to keep his promise. Clara had been with Mary almost a month.

The initial plan was that Clara was only going to stay for two or three weeks!

As he turned the corner to his house, his white colonial with black shutters came into view. A new thought dawned on him. *What am I thinking? How can I have forgotten to call Darcy? Maybe she'll have some ideas on how to tell Mom the news.*

Robert hadn't spoken with his sister in a couple of weeks; he needed to bring her into the loop. The first week that their mother had been with Mary, they had spoken often, but their phone conversations had dropped off since then. Darcy was busy at work, as was Robert.

The house was empty when he got home. Leaving his keys and briefcase on the front hall table, he kicked off his shoes, loosened his tie, and unbuttoned his light-blue shirt.

Jean had left him a note on the kitchen counter. He picked it up and read it.

> Hi, honey. The kids and I have gone food shopping. I'll bring something home for dinner. Just relax. We should be home by six.
>
> Love you,
> Jean

P.S. Darcy called and wants you to call her. She's heading to South Port to see Clara and wants to know if you want to come. I was wondering if maybe the kids and I could go along for the weekend with you and Darcy.

Robert smiled to himself. *Great minds think alike.*

Heading straight for the refrigerator for that nice cold beer he'd been promising himself all afternoon, Robert took one full swig before going into the living room to relax. He was tired. Getting away for the weekend sounded good.

Dropping himself in the recliner in the den, he reached for the lever on the side of the chair and let out a sigh as his legs and feet popped up, switching him automatically into relaxed mode. He reached for the TV remote and clicked to his favorite news network.

His ears perked up when he heard the anchor talk about an elderly woman who had wandered off from an adult daycare facility in South Port and had been missing for several hours. He was amazed; South Port never made the news.

He sat forward, wondering if it was the same day care center that his mother went to. He couldn't help thinking, *I hope they find the poor woman. That could be my mother,* even though he knew that Clara was safe and secure with Mary.

The anchor continued, "If anyone knows the whereabouts of Florence Foster, you are asked to please contact the South Port police department."

Florence? Now, wasn't that the name of the person Mother had said was her new friend? Robert thought. *No, that'd be too much of a coincidence,* he reasoned. But he wasn't sure.

Clicking off the television, he took a deep breath, wanting to rid himself of the chatter and stress. He just wanted to relax. He closed his eyes, then instantly opened them again. He'd forgotten to call Darcy.

Reaching for the phone on the table next to him, he dialed the number. After three rings, he began preparing himself to leave a message on her answering machine. But then he heard Darcy's voice.

"Hey, you're home for a change, sis. How are you?"

"Good, Robert. How are you doing?"

"I'm tired."

"Me too," Darcy said with a sigh. "Funny you should call. I was going to call you this evening, to see if you wanted to go to visit Mom this weekend. It's her birthday, you know."

"Yes, and Mary's too. They're planning their annual birthday celebration."

"Mother's been on my mind lately. I've been so busy at work I feel like I've been neglecting her. Let's surprise her and Mary with something really special. I'll put on my thinking cap."

"She's been on my mind, too. Yes, let's do something special, especially since Mary won't take any money from us." Then his tone changed. "You know, we need to move Mom back home. I've been dreading it. She and Mary have been enjoying each other, but it isn't fair to Mary. We need to keep our promise and return Mom to her own house."

"I've been thinking the same thing," Darcy said. "Do you want to move her this weekend?"

Robert was silent for a moment, "Okay, let's do it," he sighed. "I'll call Mary and let her know we'll be coming and plan to tell Mom as a family. Jean and the kids are coming, too. We'll all stay with Mom at Mary's. That way we're not making her go home right away. It'll give her some time to get used to the idea. She'll need it, I'm sure, and I know Mary won't mind. She is always inviting us to stay at her house. We'll have to talk about some safety concerns, too."

"Like what?" Darcy asked.

"Like all of us checking in on her on a daily basis. We need to make sure she's taking her medication and eating right. We could hire someone to do it, like home-care nurses from a private agency. It would take the burden off us, and off Mary, too."

"That sounds like a good idea, but we should talk with Mary and look at all the options before we jump into anything. Mom may not like the idea of some stranger coming in. We have to include her in the decision-making process. If she isn't on board with the idea, it may backfire on us."

"Right you are. It will be a family decision, with all of us involved, including Mary."

Robert asked Darcy if she had heard the news about a woman who wandered off from the senior center in South Port that afternoon. He knew Darcy got the local hometown news off her computer every day.

"No," Darcy said. "I haven't had time to turn on my computer yet. I was just walking in when I heard the phone ringing."

"Turn on the news," Robert suggested. "The woman's name is Florence. I'm worried it might be Mom's friend."

"I hope they find her, whether she's Mom's new friend or not," Darcy said. Then she changed the topic. "Robert, I've got something I want to talk to you about. I'm involved with someone who is ... well, he's married. Whatever you do, don't say anything to Mom about it. She wouldn't like it. I told Mary and swore her to secrecy."

Robert was quiet for a moment. "I hope you know what you're getting yourself into, Darcy," he said carefully.

"It's not what you're thinking, Robert," Darcy said defensively. "His wife is one nasty person. They haven't gotten along for years, but neither will she give him a divorce. She just wants to make his life miserable, as miserable as hers is. Jeffrey won't force the issue because she's sick."

"What's wrong with her?"

"She's got a bipolar disorder," Darcy said matter-of-factly.

Darcy dropped the subject. Her timing was off; she knew Robert was getting upset with her news about being involved with Jeff. She was sure she could talk to him about it at some other time. Persuasion was her specialty, and she hoped Robert would give her some pointers on how to handle the situation. "What time are you getting to South Port tomorrow?" she asked, changing the subject.

"I told Mary I'd be there before noon. You?"

"Not much later. Gotta run. See you then."

"Darcy," Robert said before hanging up, "I love you."

"I love you, too. Thanks for all you do," she added. "I wish I could be as involved with Mom as you are. But my job is so demanding and—"

Robert cut her short. "Darcy, stop beating yourself up. You do what you can."

Robert hung up the phone and leaned back in the chair. One thing he knew for sure: Darcy didn't have to worry about him telling their mother. It would break her heart if she ever found out.

Chapter Twenty-Nine

In Way Over Her Head

DARCY STEPPED OUT OF the shower and changed into a black velour sweat suit. It felt good to be in comfortable clothing after a long day at work.

She wanted to relax, but she couldn't think straight. Her head was spinning and she felt confused. She grabbed a bottle of water from the refrigerator, flopped on the couch, and started tapping her fingers to the beat of the music coming from the radio.

Taking a big swig of water, she glanced around her spacious, elegantly furnished condo, wishing she had someone to talk to. She loved her home, but it felt empty. She needed someone in her life to share it with. Her mother had been right about one thing: it was time for her to settle down and marry. She was readier than she'd ever been, but couldn't let her mother know just how ready she really was. She didn't want to give her any more fuel to nag her about getting married.

After she'd gotten off the phone with Robert, she called Jeff to tell him she would be going to see her mother this weekend. "What's it to me?" he asked, rather coldly, she thought. "You know I've got plans to be out of town on business," he said. They argued over when he'd be able to see her again. He wasn't sure and wouldn't commit to seeing her the following weekend.

"I'm tired of being the other woman," she suddenly screamed into the phone. "Who's it going to be, me or her?" She slammed the phone down, without allowing him time to get another word in.

Darcy got up and poured herself a glass of wine. The water was refreshing, but she needed something stronger to calm her. *Why can't he leave his wife, if he truly loves me? He's told me so often enough. It's been a year and he still says he can't leave Stella. He has to wait for the "right time."*

Jeff was now saying that Stella's bipolar disorder was worse than ever, that she was always agitated and moody these days; most nights she couldn't sleep more than two or three hours. To make matters worse, he and Stella argued constantly over her spending too much money, on clothes and anything else she happened to want. Clearly, she was in a manic phase, he'd told Darcy. He couldn't prove it, but he suspected that she'd stopped taking her meds. "Now is not the time to talk to her about divorce," he'd told her. "Believe me, when she's like this she can be unreasonable. As a matter of fact, she can be downright vicious."

Darcy believed him, but she was growing weary. Stella's illness could keep him from ever leaving her. She had to force him to make a decision: her or Stella. Stella could survive without Jeff, but Darcy couldn't. She needed him.

At that moment Darcy hated Stella. She was ruining her life. She put the half-empty glass of wine down on the coffee table and slumped back on the couch.

She had an idea. If Jeff ever found out, he'd be angry with her or, even worse, leave her. She didn't care; she'd have to risk it. The holidays would be coming soon enough. She couldn't bear to spend another Christmas or New Year's without him.

The wine calmed her; she could feel warmth and relaxation begin to creep into her body. She stared at the phone sitting beside her. All she had to do was to dial the number she'd found in the phone book.

She'd rehearsed what she would say to Stella for quite some time: "I've been seeing Jeff for a year. It's me he's in love with, not you. Give him the divorce he's been begging you for. It's over between you and him, and you know it."

Darcy bit her bottom lip. She was feeling desperate, and was beginning to question whether she actually had the courage to call Stella. She had no one she could call and talk to about it. None of her friends knew about Jeffrey. She'd had to keep it quiet all this time. He'd insisted on it. He said it was too risky.

Darcy had to agree with him, but for a different reason. She knew her friends would try to talk her out of seeing him. *They'd tell me I'm in over my head. How could they know that he's mad about me? None of them would understand, even if I told them how good he is to me. I certainly have enough expensive gifts to prove it,* she thought with growing bitterness.

But now she had shared her secret with Mary and Robert. She couldn't wait for the day they would finally get to meet him. Then they'd see for themselves how wonderful he was.

Darcy could feel the strength of his warm embrace. She loved how his green eyes pierced her when they were making love, how his salt-and-pepper hair fell to one side, almost covering his right eye. He was handsome and intelligent, and rich. What more could a girl hope for? At least Robert and Mary hadn't said hateful things when she told them. *They could have told me I'm nuts,* she thought.

Of course, she could never tell Mother. She'd never understand someone having an affair. The only man she'd ever been with in her life was her father. She couldn't understand why or how she stayed with him all those years. Even though he was sick with depression and couldn't help it, living with him all those years must have been terrible. *Poor Mother,* Darcy thought. *She's led such a sad life being the dutiful wife. I want my life to be different. I want love and romance.*

Darcy finished her glass of wine and decided to have another. She needed courage to call Stella. If she didn't do it now, she might never dare make that call. Someday Jeff would thank her for doing what he could not. They could get on with their lives. Stella would give him a divorce; they could make wedding plans. She wanted the biggest wedding anyone had ever seen. She finished her second glass of wine, placed the empty glass on the table, and dialed the number.

"Hello," a woman's voice answered, sounding sleepy. Darcy quickly glanced over at the clock on the wall. It was nine o'clock. *How did it get so late? I shouldn't be calling now,* she thought, her panic rising.

"Is this Stella?" she asked, summoning all the nerve she could, trying to sound pleasant at the same time.

"Yes. Who is this?" Darcy detected annoyance in her voice.

"My name is Darcy Lewis. I'm sorry to call so late. I didn't realize—"

Stella cut her short. "What do you want?"

"I wondered if Jeffrey had ... told you anything about me," Darcy said hesitantly.

"What are you talking about? Is this some kind of a prank call?"

"Please," Darcy said, "don't hang up. I need to talk to you."

"Okay." Stella still sounded annoyed. "What is it you're calling about?" she snapped. "Get to the point!"

"Jeffrey and I are having an affair. I know he's tried many times to tell you about us, but he didn't want to hurt you. Jeffrey's in love with me. We've been seeing each other for a year now."

A brief silence. "Even if Jeffrey did have an affair with you, Darcy, whoever you are," Stella said, her voice suddenly slow and deep and hard as steel, "you're not the only one he's having an affair with. Do you know that?"

There was more silence before Darcy could answer. "Jeffrey's in love with me," she countered, anger slipping into her voice.

"Yes, he's in love with you," Stella said wearily. "You, and I can't count how many others."

"That's nonsense," Darcy dismissed. "He wants to marry me. You're just saying that because you're jealous."

"I'm not jealous in the least. In fact, the truth is that I'm the one who wants the divorce. I wish I could get rid of him. He's a liar and a cheat. We haven't slept in the same room with each other for years. Our relationship was over years ago. We share the same house, that's all. It's just a marriage of convenience — *his* convenience."

Darcy was struck silent.

"Let me tell you something, honey," Stella continued. "Your Jeffrey will never divorce me because he loves money—*my* money. We signed a prenuptial that if we ever divorced, he wouldn't get one red cent of my fortune. So, he does what he wants and I do what I want."

"You're lying!" Darcy yelled. "He won't divorce you because of your illness."

"And what illness would that be?"

"You know perfectly well what illness I am talking about, Stella," Darcy snorted. "Your bipolar disorder." Darcy was standing with the phone in one hand and her third drink in the other.

Stella roared with laughter. "That's the best one I've heard yet," she said when she finished laughing.

"I guess I'm just a walking medical disaster. Let's see, I've had cancer and MS, now it's a bipolar disorder, eh? Do yourself a big favor, honey. Get rid of him."

Darcy slammed the phone down. She couldn't believe what she just heard. Her face was red and streaked with tears. *I don't believe her. She's lying. Jeffrey would never use or abuse me that way. He loves me. I know he does,* she thought with a moan.

She dialed Jeffrey's cell, hoping she could catch him before he left for the weekend. When his answering machine picked up, she snapped her cell phone closed. She didn't want to leave a message. There was nothing she could do now except wait for him to call her.

She was sure he could straighten everything out. Stella was lying; it was as simple as that. Throwing her head back, she emptied her third glass of wine. She should eat something, she knew, but the idea of food didn't interest her. She wanted to sleep and wake up in the morning to the sound of Jeffrey's voice, laughing at all the lies Stella had told her.

Chapter Thirty

Search for a Missing Person

MARY STOPPED WORKING ON the cookie dough she'd been making, wiped her hands on her green print apron, and answered the phone. It was Robert. He quickly filled her in on what he knew about a missing person from the center. "Have you seen the news?" he asked.

"No, I was busy getting ready for the weekend," Mary told him.

A few minutes later, Mary turned on the television just in time to hear the tail end of the news. It *was* Florence they were looking for. She was glad Robert had called her.

She decided not to disturb Clara, who was in her room taking a nap. She knew Clara would be worried sick when she heard about poor Florence.

Glancing at her watch she saw that it was almost four. She decided to try her luck calling the center, just in case someone was still there who could tell her something more about Florence. She dialed the number. After the fourth ring, the answering machine came on. She left a message for Rebecca, the program director, to call her as soon as possible.

She went back to work on her cookies and tried not to think of Florence. Her thoughts quickly turned to the issue of Clara returning to her home. Mary had mixed feelings about it. On the one hand, she wanted Clara to be happy and safe back in her own home. On the other hand, she wasn't so sure Clara could care for herself. She could handle the small tasks Mary asked of her, like setting the table and cleaning up after meals, but actually preparing meals was another matter. She thought about the afternoon Clara decided to surprise her with a meatloaf. It was a disaster! Once they sat down at the table to eat it, Clara was so embarrassed at how it had turned out, she promised not to try it again. Mary told her a little white lie about it being not so bad, but the fact was, it was absolutely terrible. She'd put way too much salt in it, and used cornmeal instead of bread crumbs.

Mary knew that living with her had done Clara a world of good, not to mention the vitamins and good home-cooked meals. She didn't want to see her end up in the same isolated situation again by going home too soon.

The shrill sound of the ringing phone brought Mary back from her daydreaming. Wiping the cookie dough off her hands again, she picked up the phone and recognized the sound of Rebecca's voice instantly. Mary asked her if there was any word yet about Florence.

"Actually, no," Rebecca told her, "but I'm staying here at the center calling as many people as I can in the hopes that someone knows anything about her whereabouts." Mary could hear the tension in her voice.

"I was on the phone calling people when you tried to get through. In fact, you were next on my list of people to call. The police are doing their best to help, but no word." She told Mary that Florence had no family or friends around, and her son lived in Florida. "He is beside himself with worry," she added. Rebecca knew Florence and Clara had become friendly, and was hoping Clara might know something. It seems Florence had left right after Mary and Clara.

Mary told Rebecca she would wake Clara from her nap and tell her what happened and ask her if Florence may have said anything to her about going somewhere.

Mary hung up the phone, deeply concerned. This was serious.

Before Mary could wake Clara, she heard the water running in the bathroom and knew Clara was awake. She sat at the kitchen table and waited for her to come down. When she did, she seemed startled by Mary's expression.

"Mary, my goodness," Clara said. "You look worried. Whatever is the matter?"

"Sit down, honey. I need to tell you something." Clara sat down at the table and placed her hand on top of Mary's.

"Clara, did Florence mention anything to you about planning on going anywhere other than home after she left the center?" Mary asked her.

"Why do you ask?" Clara asked, surprised. "Mary, is Florence alright?"

"We don't know. She left the center right after we left and didn't tell anyone where she was going. I was just on the phone with Rebecca. She wanted me to ask you if Florence told you anything. It's been on the news that she's been missing since she left the community center."

Clara scratched her head and shook it, as if trying to clear the cobwebs. Sitting quietly, she didn't answer right away. Mary politely gave her time to think. She could see that Clara was trying desperately to search her brain. When Clara broke the silence, there were tears in her eyes.

"What is it, Clara?" Mary asked, alarmed. "Why are you crying?"

"I know something has happened to her," was all Clara could say.

"Maybe not," Mary said hopefully. "She could be visiting with someone."

"No, I think she's lost."

"Why do you say that?" Mary questioned her. "Did she tell you she was going somewhere? This is important, Clara. Try to think. Can you remember what the two of you talked about today?"

"Well, we always talk about so many things. We've got a lot in common, you know."

"Yes, I know. You've told me."

"She used to live somewhere in this neighborhood," Clara said, the thought trailing away.

"Did the two of you talk about the neighborhood then?"

"I ... I don't remember, Mary. I'm just no help, am I?" Clara said sadly.

"It's okay, Clara. She'll show up," Mary said, trying to sound optimistic. "A lot of people are out looking for her."

"Poor Florence," Clara moaned. "I feel terrible. I wish I could remember what we talked about."

Mary got up and put her arms around her. She needed a hug.

Suddenly Clara grabbed Mary's hand and squeezed it. "Mary," she said excitedly, "I think I remember something." Clara got up from the chair and the two friends stood facing each other, their hands locked in each other's, their eyes fixed on one another.

Clara took a deep breath and began. "She asked me if I would like to visit her old neighborhood sometime. She said it was on Hancock Street, and it was the house she grew up in. She got so excited when I told her I would love to. Then I asked her if she would like to visit me. She said she couldn't think of anything she would like to do more. When you picked me up yesterday, she started to come with me and I told her that she couldn't come immediately, but maybe another time. I told her to stay and wait for the van with the others for her ride home. I could tell she was disappointed, but she said okay, and went back to sit on the couch to wait for the van to take her home. Maybe she's either trying to find her old home on Hancock Street or us. What do you think?"

"Well, I guess it's a possibility," Mary said. "We should at least let Rebecca know. She could have the police scout both neighborhoods."

Mary quickly called Rebecca and gave her Clara's news. Rebecca said she'd pass the information on to the police immediately and thanked Mary. "And please thank Clara for her help." Rebecca added that the van driver said he dropped her off at her usual stop. "Any ideas about her whereabouts are a big help."

As she hung up, Mary had an idea. She stopped working on the cookie dough, covered it with a moist cloth, and set it in the refrigerator. Then she grabbed her purse. "Come on, Clara, let's go."

"Go where?" Clara asked, puzzled, as she followed Mary to the back door.

"We can't just sit here making cookies while Florence is lost," Mary said. "Let's drive around the neighborhood. I'll need your help. Maybe we'll get lucky and find her. You have to come with me. No telling what shape she'll be in."

"You're a genius, Mary!" Clara exclaimed. They walked out the back door arm in arm, matching looks of seriousness written on their faces. The sun had begun to set. Time was running out. Darkness would soon set in. They meant business; they were on a mission.

Chapter Thirty-One

The Rescue

MARY KEPT UP A stream of chatter as they drove around the neighborhood. She wanted to give Clara something to think about other than Florence. "I forgot to tell you, dear, that Robert called while you were sleeping. Not only is he coming up this weekend, but so are Jean and your grandchildren. Oh, and he said that Darcy's coming, too," Mary added. "I'm already making a list of things I need to pick up at the store. I'm going to make a big pot of American chop suey. It's one of Robert and Darcy's favorites, as I recall. And homemade bread fresh from the oven, and salad. And an apple pie for dessert. I'm also making chocolate chip cookies for everyone."

Mary kept the conversation rolling, hoping to help calm Clara's anxiety as they slowly drove up one street and down another on their way to Hancock Street. When they were about to pass Nellie's General Store, Mary had an idea. She pulled up in front, parked, and motioned that Clara should remain in the car. Nellie's was a town landmark. It had been part of the neighborhood for more than thirty years, and everyone frequented it from time to time for last-minute necessities.

The bell hanging over the door rang as Mary entered the store and walked over to the counter where Nellie, a stout woman close to Mary's age, was bagging the last of a customer's groceries. Waiting patiently for her turn, Mary glanced around to see if anyone else was in the store. She was so busy looking around that she didn't see Nellie's customer gather up her bags and leave, so she was startled by Nellie's greeting. "Hello, Mary. What can I do for you today?"

"Hi, Nellie," she answered, quickly gathering her thoughts. "I'm not here to buy anything today. I'm actually looking for someone and was hoping maybe you could help me."

A look of obvious annoyance settled across Nellie's features. "Oh. I'll try. Who you looking for?" she asked brusquely.

"Her name's Florence. She goes to the same day care Clara goes to. She's been missing since early today. I have reason to believe that she may be lost somewhere in the neighborhood."

Nellie sighed. "Oh dear. That doesn't sound good. What does she look like?" Nellie set to fussing with some papers on the counter and did not look up. *You never know what kind of a mood you're going to find Nellie in,* Mary thought. *She can go from nice to nasty in the blink of an eye.*

"She's short and stout. Personally, I think she looks a bit like she could be married to Santa Claus," Mary chuckled, "except that she has red hair."

"That helps," Nellie interrupted querulously.

Mary continued patiently. "She wears brown-rimmed glasses, and uses a cane."

"Then she couldn't have walked far, if she uses a cane," Nellie said with a huff. "Any idea what she's wearing that would help identify her?"

Mary shook her head, thinking for a moment. She knew she was treading on thin ice. Nellie was slipping into her awful self; she could hear it in her voice.

"Well, I haven't seen her here," Nellie said, still not looking up from what she was doing. "Do the police know about this?"

"Oh, yes," Mary said. "They're patrolling the neighborhood as we speak."

Nellie finally put down the papers on her counter and looked up at Mary, her hands on her hips. "I don't understand how someone could get themselves lost. If I were you, Mary, I'd go home and let the police do their job."

Mary could feel the muscles in her neck knot up; the rise and fall of her chest began to quicken. "First of all, Nellie," she said, measuring out her words carefully, "You are *not* me, and, secondly, I can't just sit around doing nothing like some people."

"You don't have to be rude, Mary," Nellie said haughtily. "It's starting to get dark. You're not going to find her in the dark."

Mary could feel the temperature rising on her face. She squeezed her lips tightly to keep from saying a word and turned around to leave. It was just like Nellie to not care about a lonely, old woman wandering around the streets, lost.

Nellie came from behind the counter and started to follow Mary, who quickened her steps toward the door. Before Nellie could say another word, Mary yelled over her shoulder, as loudly as she could while still walking towards the door, "If you happen to see her, Nellie, call the police, would you? I don't want to lose any more of the daylight. Have a good evening," she added as she closed the door behind her with a bang, not giving Nellie a chance to reply.

Nellies head snapped back just in time to keep the door from hitting her in the face. "Well, wasn't that rude! What's got into her?" Nellie wondered aloud as she pulled down the shade and placed the CLOSED sign in the window.

Mary slammed the car door and started the engine.

Clara could see she was upset. "No luck?" Clara asked.

"Not a bit," Mary said angrily. "You know how Nellie can be sometimes. If I weren't a Christian woman, I'd tell her a thing or two. Put her right in her place. It's too bad no one ever tells her what they think of her."

"What did she say that's got you so upset?"

"All Nellie could say was, 'Let the police look for her.' She suggested I go home before it got dark. She seemed not to care about Florence one bit. I let her know I wasn't going to sit around while a lost, old woman was out wandering the streets. God only knows what might happen to her all alone. It's getting colder by the minute. She could freeze to death out here."

"Good for you, Mary," Clara declared. "I'm glad you told her how you felt. Too bad you didn't just slam the door in her face."

"I did!" Mary admitted, and both she and Clara enjoyed a good laugh. Then silence returned as they went on with their hunt. They were determined to find Florence.

They lingered longer than necessary at stop signs and intersections, looking up and down streets. But after over an hour of searching, Florence was still nowhere to be found. Clara sat stiffly, her fingers interlaced with each other. Her palms were moist. If they didn't find Florence, the police would have to.

Mary glanced at the clock on the dashboard. She knew that she only had a few more minutes until darkness fell, which would make finding Florence just that much more difficult. They decided to drive over to the neighborhood on Hancock Street again.

Mary turned the car around and headed for Hancock Street, only a few blocks away. Within minutes she was pulling up in front of the house Florence said used to be her home. This time they parked and both Mary and Clara started to get out. Mary stopped to reach into the glove compartment for a flashlight.

They could see from where they were standing that the house was dark. It looked deserted. They slowly headed up the path to the front door. Several shutters were either missing or falling off the small, rustic cape, which was badly in need of a paint job.

Once at the door, Mary knocked once, then twice. When there was no answer, she tried to open the door, but found it was locked. They went around to the back of the house and searched the backyard. Both could see that several planks were missing from the porch deck and that one side of the porch railing had broken off and was lying on the ground. The deck was empty except for a small, dirty white plastic table and chair set that lay on its side. It looked like the wind had played havoc with it.

"Stay here a minute, Clara," Mary suggested. "I want to get a better look." Mary carefully climbed the porch stairs and tried the back door. It too was locked. Noticing a window, she held her breath and tried to open it. No luck.

It was locked tight. Cupping her hands tightly around both eyes, she pressed her face to the window to get a better look. Her nose flattened as she peeked inside.

There was just enough light from a nearby street-light for her eyes to scan the inside of the kitchen. The room was empty, the house uninhabited. *If she did find her way here, she probably left depressed realizing she couldn't get in what used to be her home. Poor thing,* thought Mary.

"Any luck?" Clara yelled from the bottom of the porch step, her arms wrapped around herself in an attempt to keep warm.

"No luck. The place is deserted, locked up tighter than a drum." Mary jumped and almost lost her footing as a calico cat appeared out of nowhere and came racing past her.

"Come down from there before you fall," Clara yelled.

Mary came down and they found themselves standing under a tall sycamore tree in the center of the yard, staring up at the dark, deserted house. Mary put her hand on Clara's shoulder, wanting to comfort her. She could see the disappointment and concern on her friend's face. Their hope was fading. There was no one in sight. Silence filled the air like dense fog. In the distance they could hear the faint sound of a fire engine. Clara and Mary looked at each other. There was no need to speak; their sad expressions spoke for them. It was over. The search had ended.

Defeated, they turned to leave.

"Wait, Mary," Clara said, abruptly grabbing her arm. In the corner of the property was a small, dilapidated shed. They hadn't noticed it when they'd entered the yard, having come from the opposite direction. A number of roof shingles were missing, and it looked like it would take several coats of white paint and some patching here and there to restore the shed to any semblance of usefulness.

They walked across the yard and over to the shed. The door was unlatched and slightly ajar. Mary slowly pushed it open. It creaked noisily on its rusty hinges. Turning on the flashlight, she carefully searched along the walls for any sign of life. The flashlight stopped at what looked like a big bundle wrapped in black plastic. Mary stepped into the shed and with her free hand touched the object. To her shock, it moved slowly.

Mary jumped, quickly jerking back her hand. She saw a woman's leg uncurl, then another.

"Florence, is that you?" Mary yelled from a safe distance. The flashlight came to rest on two weary, big brown eyes staring back at her.

"It's about time someone got here," Florence's voice answered, raspy and tired. "I'm hungry. And cold."

Florence was a chatterbox all the way back home. She was happy, not only to be out of the cold but also to be with Clara and Mary. Mary wanted to question her, but she knew it wasn't the time. Both she and Clara would have plenty of time to find out what had happened later. She just wanted to get Florence back to her house, get some food and a hot cup of tea into her, then bed her down for the night.

She knew she had to contact the police and Rebecca right away to let them know Florence was safe. She was sure Rebecca would call Florence's son to tell him the good news. Mary thought it would be best if Rebecca gave Florence's son her phone number. Hopefully, he would be okay with his mother staying for the night. Maybe Dr. Hoyt should take a look at her in the morning if Florence's son would be okay with it; she seemed fine but Mary wanted reassurance. For now, what Florence needed was TLC, warmth, food, and rest.

With both of her guests sound asleep, Mary lay in bed staring up at the ceiling. She was finding it difficult to sleep. Her mind kept going back to Florence and her sad eyes when Mary had told her she would take her home in the morning.

"Could I stay here with you and Clara for the party?" she had asked.

"Why, yes, Florence. That's fine with me." The answer had flown out of her before she realized it. It hadn't occurred to her that Florence may want to stay longer than the party. For now, it was nice that she was safe and happy.

Chapter Thirty-Two

Housemates

MARY WAS UP EARLY, delighted with the thought of making a nice, big breakfast for everyone. Sitting at the kitchen table sipping a cup of hot coffee, she found herself humming an old gospel hymn to herself.

She bowed her head and closed her eyes, and thanked God for Florence, happy that she'd been found safe. "The Lord is so wonderful. Why do we worry?" she asked aloud. "Yes, Lord, and you're always right on time."

She was still deep in prayer when the phone rang. She jumped up quickly, hoping to answer it before the ringing woke Clara or Florence. It was Paul.

"I'm sorry I haven't called you sooner. I didn't get in till late last night, but it was way too late to call then and disturb you. I was away on business. Mary, I am so happy you found Mother, and I can't thank you enough for letting her spend the night. I couldn't believe she found her way to the old house."

Mary told him the whole story of how she and Clara found her. "It was pretty amazing," Mary agreed.

"The whole thing is a miracle," Paul said, "and I have you to thank for it. My plan is to fly up to New England as soon as possible and decide what must be done for Mother. I guess it's pretty clear that she can't live alone anymore."

Before Paul could continue, Mary cut him short. "Paul, I want you to know that Florence is no trouble. In fact, I was going to ask you if I could keep her here with Clara and myself, at least over the weekend." She hurried to sell the idea before he could come up with an objection. "Clara's son and daughter are on their way here to spend the weekend, and we're all looking forward to a good time. It's Clara's and my birthday party. Florence would enjoy it, and it'll be a great way for her to forget what's happened. I have plenty of room here. I know you don't know me from a hole in the ground, but I have references, and ..."

This time Paul cut *her* off. "Mary, please, you don't have to explain who you are. I've heard nothing but wonderful things about you from folks at the center. I got a call from someone there last night—the director of the program, I believe, and she sang your praises. If you're sure she won't be a bother," Paul added.

"Just the opposite. She'll add a lot to the festivities."

"Well, I *am* swamped with work. If I could come up Monday, I would be most grateful. I plan to pay you for your generosity." Mary let that pass. "In the meantime, I plan to start making some calls to try to find a place for my mother. I've been dreading this day for years, but the time has finally come. I would bring Mother back here, but I know that she'd never want that. She may get confused once in a while, but she has always been clear with where she wants to live. I promised her years ago that she could live out her days in South Port."

"Florence is such a nice woman and really, dear, I am more than happy to have her here," Mary reassured him. "I'm going to take her back to her apartment later on today so she can get some clothes and whatever else she needs. I'm assuming you'll let the rest of your family know that she is okay."

"I'm afraid there is no other family, Mary. It's just Mother and me."

"Oh dear," Mary sighed. "Poor Florence. No wonder she was so excited about staying for the party this weekend. I can see she loves people."

Mary wrapped up the conversation with Paul. She hung up the phone, pulled the sash a little tighter on her bathrobe, and sat back down to finish her cup of coffee. She found herself wondering how Paul could leave his mother so alone and so unconnected to people. She also knew it was unkind of her to pass judgement on someone. But, with the exception of the senior center, she seemed to have no connection to anyone else locally.

"I don't think there's anything worse than being lonely when you're old, except being lonely and sick," Mary mused. "I don't want to be alone. There, now, I've said it out loud." Mary stood up and stared out the window.

Well, now you've managed to surprise yourself, Mary Thomas! Though it wasn't the first time she'd thought about it; in fact, she'd been thinking it for some time now. It had been a gripping fear that held her hostage and challenged her to make a decision.

She knew she had to plan for her future. What would she do with her house? Where would she live if she had to leave? She didn't want to live in a nursing home any more than Florence and Clara did.

She wanted to live in a homelike atmosphere, someplace that felt like a home. She wanted to smell home-cooked meals in the oven and feel like part of a family. Mary repeated the word *family* again out loud, and then again. *Family.* That was the key word.

Clara instinctively created her own family with her stuffed animals and dolls when she felt alone. They became her family in the attic. Mary wanted more than anything in the world to open her house to a few people who, like her, didn't want to live alone. She felt her home was a perfect place for a community. It would be a dream come true if Clara and Florence could stay with her.

Just at that moment Clara stepped into the kitchen, interrupting Mary's train of thought. Mary jumped at the sound of her voice.

"Good morning, Clara! How did you sleep?"

"Like a log, thanks. How about you?"

"Pretty well, once I finally got to sleep," Mary admitted.

∞

Clara poured herself a cup of coffee and sat down at the table. "To tell you the truth, Mary, I have a lot on my mind myself. I know the kids are going to discuss my going back home. I'm ready to go. I've stayed here with you way longer than expected. I can't begin to thank you for all you've done for me." Clara smiled over her cup of coffee. "Mary, I need to admit to something. Something I've been keeping to myself for too long. I couldn't, and wouldn't, admit it to myself, but now I can tell you this."

Pausing, she placed her hand on top of Mary's. "I don't ever want to live alone again." She stopped to let the idea sink in. "Being here with you, I've realized how lonely I've been since Frank died. I'm going to tell the children I'm prepared to start looking for a retirement home. I have to make these changes in my life. I don't want to be a burden to the children." Clara sat back, a huge weight lifted from her mind.

"Clara," Mary responded, smiling broadly, "I am glad you felt you could share that with me. I know that it took courage to come to that decision. I have something I want to share with you as well. Something that I've come to terms with too."

Mary took a deep breath. "Since you've been here with me, I have felt more alive than I've felt in years, and I know why I feel this way. It's because you've been here with me. I never knew until now that I've been lonely too. I don't want to be alone any more than you do." Clara looked like she could be knocked over with a feather.

"The difference is," Mary plowed on, "I know I could never leave this house, so a retirement home is out of the question for me. But I also know that this place is much too big for one person. I can hardly keep it up any more. This home has always needed people in it. Clara, I've been thinking, and well ... would you be interested in living here with me?"

"You mean, forever?"

"Yes, forever, if you want. That's right, Clara. We'd be housemates."

As the two friends sat facing each other, Clara stretched her hands out to Mary, who caught them in her own. Tears flowed freely from their eyes. They were both overwhelmed with happiness.

"Mary, this just may be the happiest day of my life," Clara said when she could. "Thank you. Thank you for being so generous. Of course, I will pay my share, and there will be no discussion about that. I am quite able to."

"We can work all that out this weekend, dear Clara," Mary said, "when your children are here."

"Won't they be surprised! I know they were planning for me to go back home. We can surprise them with our new plans. You know something, Mary?" Clara asked with a twinkle in her still-moist eyes.

"What's that, Clara?"

"This is the best birthday present you could have ever given me." And Clara burst into tears all over again.

Mary reached up behind her for the Kleenex box on the kitchen counter and set it between them. They each took one and blew their noses in unison. "You've been through so much, what with Frank passing away and then you're getting sick and having to go into the hospital."

The thought of Clara's hospitalization made Mary decide that it might be wise to test the water, just to be sure that Clara really was over the worst of her problems. "Do you miss the dolls and Teddy at all, Clara?" she asked cautiously.

"What dolls and Teddy are you talking about?" Clara asked, suddenly puzzled.

Mary groaned. "Don't you remember the dolls, Clara?" she asked gently. "You took them with you everywhere."

Clara tried to keep a straight face but couldn't. She began to laugh.

"Oh, Clara Palmer Lewis, you about scared me out of my wits!" Mary said angrily, then burst into laughter herself. "For a minute there you had me convinced that you'd lost your memory again."

"No, Mary," Clara managed in spite of her laughter, "I don't ever even think of the dolls and Teddy. No, actually that's not true. I have given them a moment's thought."

Mary could not have been happier to hear those words from Clara's mouth. The dolls and Teddy were history.

Florence entered the kitchen and was standing in the doorway. "Well, now, what's all this?" she asked good-naturedly.

They both turned. Still holding on to each other's hand, Mary said, "Oh, good morning, Florence. We were just feeling blessed to have each other. How did you sleep?"

"Wonderfully," Florence said with a smile. "I woke up smelling the coffee. Can I get a mug?"

"For years Clara and I have been choosing mugs that go along with our mood. I thought you might like this one," Mary said, handing the mug to her.

Florence poured herself a cup of coffee and smiled at the words, which simply read, "Life Without Friends Is No Life at All."

"So, what in the world are you two so happy about?" Florence asked.

"Can I tell her, Mary?"

"Sure. She'll be the third person to know."

"Mary and I are going to be housemates!"

Chapter Thirty-Three

The Dolls

FLORENCE SAT AT THE table, wrapped in one of Mary's floor-length bathrobes, her soft hair tousled from a good night's sleep. She was stunned by what they'd told her. "But I thought you *were* housemates," she stammered, half-smiling.

"Well, yes, we have been housemates," Mary interjected, "but it was only supposed to be temporary, for a few weeks."

"Oh, I see," Florence said, slowly processing the information. "I guess I thought that you ... just take people in ... when they need a home, like you took me in."

Florence took a sip of her coffee, set it down before her, then studied the spoon she'd just used to stir it. It felt good to be sitting with Mary and Clara. She didn't want to think about having to leave and go home. She just wanted to enjoy her stay. She enjoyed being with people, especially Mary and Clara. She secretly longed for Mary to ask her to stay longer, but that conversation seemed out of the question. After all, they hardly even knew each other.

The conversation turned to preparations for the birthday party three days hence. Mary told Florence she'd spoken to Paul and that he was fine with the idea of her staying through the weekend. Florence was thrilled. Mary told her Paul said he would call her soon.

Florence listened with a far keener interest as they chattered on about the meal and the birthday cake decoration, now that she knew she was going to be part of the festivities. She couldn't get over how excited Mary and Clara were, like two young girls babbling and giggling on about their first school dance. She felt good being with them. They lifted her spirits. It was so much better than her empty apartment.

The phone rang, interrupting the plans for the birthday party and Florence's thoughts. It was Paul calling Mary back to tell her that he had found an assisted care home for his mother and that he would be coming on Monday to take her to her new place right there in South Port. He told her he had put a deposit down to hold the room for his mother. Mary suggested that he hold off telling his mother about it until after the birthday party.

"Frankly, Mary, if I could I'd put it off forever," Paul said candidly. "It's going to be so difficult for my mother to leave her apartment. She liked living there. A part of her is going to die with this move. I just ache for her. It was nothing like the home I was raised in, but it's been home to her for the past four years. She's been comfortable there. I know it's going to be a struggle. I'm afraid I can't see any other solution."

∞

Time was running out. The birthday party was only one day away now, and the mad rush to complete everything was on. Last-minute details were finally underway, which included cleaning the house and doing the last-minute grocery shopping.

Mary took charge like a seasoned general, delegating what needed to be done and who needed to do it. Clara and Florence were delighted to be doing what they could. The house buzzed with laughter. Euphoria engulfed the house, seeping everywhere, permeating every room like an uncontrollable, invisible fragrance.

∞

By the end of the day, all three were bone-tired. It had been a busy day. The sun began to slowly descend just as dark clouds converged to cover it.

The three women sat at the kitchen table. The night air was closing in. No one spoke. The whole house was quiet. Florence's eyes fluttered at half-mast as she sat with both elbows on the table. Clara sat with only one elbow on the table, her head resting comfortably in the palm of her hand. Looking off into space, she had nothing particular on her mind. Mary looked at the two of them and couldn't stifle a huge yawn. Neither of her companions even reacted.

The clock over the kitchen sink told her it was seven. It didn't matter. She was ready for bed and said to herself, "I can barely keep my eyes open." She smiled as she looked from one to the other of her friends. "I guess we should all think about going to bed," Mary finally said. "Tomorrow is another day, and it's going to be a busy one." When neither of them stirred, she spoke again, a little louder this time.

Clara remained still; only her eyes turned to look at Mary. "I was daydreaming again," she admitted with a sleepy grin.

"What about?" Mary asked her.

"I want to go home tomorrow, to say goodbye to my house," Clara said quietly. "It's something I need to do."

"I understand, Clara. I'm sure it's not going to be easy. You've spent a good many years there. Would you like me to come with you? Or would you like to wait and have Robert and Darcy with you?"

"No, this is something I want to do by myself."

"It's not an easy thing to do," Florence said. Mary and Clara turned to look at her.

"I thought you were snoozing," Mary said, surprised.

"I was just resting my eyes," Florence said lightly. "Saying goodbye to your things is hard. I don't have much now. My apartment is small. I had a nice home once, though. I had to sell just about everything. I remember that day like it was yesterday. I cried like a baby."

"Why did you sell it all, Florence?" Clara asked.

"I had to. It was too much for me to keep. All those things wouldn't begin to fit into my apartment. I think about certain items now and then, but I don't regret it. It happens to most of us sooner or later. One thing is certain: we can't take it with us when we die. I kept some of the smaller things I loved. But the rest of it is gone."

"You're smart, Florence," Mary said as she patted her hand. "Holding on to stuff isn't healthy. It ties us down. The idea at our age is to let go, and become free to do whatever we want. It's baggage, plain and simple. Getting old doesn't have to mean it's the end. I truly believe it's just another phase of our lives. Who knows," she joked. "Maybe someday I'll decide I need a man to help me kick up my heels."

Florence laughed, but Clara could only crack a smile. She didn't want to talk about it anymore. Right now, though, all she could think about was getting in between the sheets. She was tired. Somehow, she was able to put tomorrow out of her mind. Instead, she thought about seeing the children and grandchildren. She knew it was going to be a wonderful party.

Florence yawned, then headed for bed.

"Mary," Clara asked as they joined Florence and headed for the stairs, "Do you know where I put all the dolls and Teddy?"

Mary stopped in her tracks, turned, and stared at Clara "Why, yes, Clara. Why do you ask?"

"I just wanted to make sure I knew where they were. I've decided I'm going to give them to Sara tomorrow." Mary breathed a sigh of relief, then smiled to herself as she climbed the stairs, with Clara and Florence following close behind.

Chapter Thirty-Four

Saying Goodbye to the Ghost of Christmas Past

THE NEXT MORNING, CLARA was up early. She wanted to get over to her house before her family arrived. She crept slowly down the stairs so as not to wake Mary or Florence.

She hadn't stepped a foot inside her home for over a month. It was the longest time she'd ever been away from it, she realized. She had mixed feelings about how she would feel when she walked in. Part of her felt like the ghost of Christmas past was about to fill her with remorse. Guilt had begun to settle in.

How do you leave the place left to you by your parents? she wondered. *I promised to keep it in the family.* It seemed she had spent her life doing for everyone except herself. *What would my life have been like if I hadn't listened to my parents and married Dave?* she thought.

Another softer voice encouraged her that it was time to move along. *Time's up, Clara,* the voice nudged her. *What sense does it make to hold on to an empty house full of ghosts?*

Another part of her was the ghost of Christmas present. She remembered how lonely she had felt without her family; the dolls and Teddy had been a replacement for them. It was hard living without Frank. He held a place in her heart. Frank couldn't help being sick with depression. But still, he was hard to live with. It was the children she lived for. They gave her such joy, and still did....

Clara opened the door to her house and stepped into the kitchen. She slowly closed the door behind her, then glanced around the room. She pulled up the shade over the sink and turned on the lights. The clouds that covered the morning sky kept the sun from showing itself.

Quiet filled the house, and it smelled faintly musty from being locked up and vacant. The grandfather clock, she realized, had stopped ticking. There'd been no one to wind it.

Reaching up into the cupboard, she found the mug she planned to use. It read, "It's Better to Have Loved and Lost than Never to Have Loved at All." Then she made herself a cup of tea.

"I'm starting a new life, Frank. It's about time, don't you think?" she asked aloud. Sitting at the kitchen table, she didn't know if she wanted to laugh or cry. Her life was taking on a new aspect, and she had to admit she liked it.

First, she'd have to get rid of all the furniture, and then downsize her wardrobe. She'd keep her jewelry, of course, and give whatever she didn't want to Darcy and Jean. But then there were the important things, like pictures and photo albums and, of course, Dave's letters; she could never part with them. Finally, she would get rid of Frank's things. She could do it now. Suddenly her mind was spinning. It would take time to do all she had to do. She stopped herself. Time was something she had. There was no hurry. Going through all her personal things shouldn't—and needn't—be hurried.

She stood up and began to walk through the house that had been her home for more years than she could even remember. She stopped to admire the brass lamp that sat next to her favorite chair, and ran her fingers over its faded yellow and blue plaid material. She admired the way the tassels hung from the bottom of the lamp shade. Walking over to the mantle, she smiled at the pictures. She stopped in front of the bookcase.

Clara's tattered, dusty family bible sat on the bottom shelf. She picked it up and brought it over to a chair by the window. She wanted to look through it, as she had so many times in her life. It had belonged to her mother.

After a bit, Clara put the bible back on the shelf and headed upstairs to think about what she wanted to take with her from her bedroom. Smiling, she went to the dresser and opened the jewelry box Frank had made for her. She loved it.

She picked up the pearl necklace Frank had given her for one of their anniversaries. She twirled it around in her hand, and then replaced it. Next, she took out a pair of gold earrings the children had given her one Christmas and held them in her hand, remembering how much that had meant to her. Then she glanced around the room. Her eyes came to rest on the rocking chair in front of the window. No question, it had to come. She could never leave it behind.

She had a house full of treasures. How could she decide which ones would come with her and which ones would not? *This is going to be so much harder than I'd thought,* she admitted to herself. *Every room in the house holds memories and memorabilia.*

She sat down on her bed and closed her eyes, suddenly feeling weary. *You can't take everything with you. You must pick and choose.* She opened her eyes and glanced out the window just in time to see a cardinal perched on a limb of the old oak tree. She smiled to herself. It was a good sign.

Frank had loved cardinals. He said they were a sign of good fortune, or an old soul who has come by to pay his respects. "Is that you, Frank?" she said aloud to the cardinal. As if it could hear her, it flew down to a branch closer to the window. "It is you, isn't it, Frank," she said, startled but suddenly sure. The bird looked for all the world like it wanted to help. She decided to share her burden with the bright-eyed creature.

"Frank," she said, "I'm having a much harder time than I thought I would, trying to decide what I have to get rid of. Part of me wants to take everything. I know it's silly, but everything in this house is a part of me. I need courage to let go of these old things, Frank, even though I know that once I let go, everything will be fine. It's just that the first step is so darned hard."

Clara was suddenly flooded with unexpected emotion. *I wish I didn't feel this way about these things.* Trying to fight back tears, she shut her eyes tight, but they opened again almost immediately at the sound of the cardinal pecking at the window. "It *is* you, isn't it, Frank?" she smiled through her tears. "Frank, I need your help to get through this."

As if by magic, the name George Dunlap came to her. Clara remembered Frank telling her about him on more than one occasion. Clapping her hands, she headed downstairs. She knew what to do.

She found Frank's old address book in the desk. Her fingers flipped through the pages until she found

"George Dunlap." He was someone Frank used to call when he had things he couldn't sell in the store.

Clara held her breath and dialed the number. It picked up on the first ring.

"Hello. George here."

"George, this is Clara Lewis."

"What can I do for you, Clara?"

"Well, I want to sell the contents of my house, George. Can you help me?" When he answered in the affirmative, Clara let out a sigh of relief. Then she went on to explain that she wanted her son and daughter to be there when he came, but needed to find out when they'd be available. He said he'd look forward to hearing back from her.

Clara hung up the phone, feeling as if a tremendous weight had just been lifted from her shoulders. She knew Frank had something to do with what had just transpired. She headed back upstairs to thank that cardinal—or Frank—but it was gone.

"Thank you, Frank," she said nonetheless. "I know it was you who planted that idea in my head. I just took my first step."

As if by magic Clara suddenly felt she had the courage to let go of things. She couldn't wait to tell Mary and Florence about the cardinal and her plans of emptying out the house.

∞

Mary and Florence were busy cooking in preparation for the party when Clara walked into the kitchen.

"Well," Mary said, "here's our early riser. How'd it go?"

"At first I struggled with what I was about to do," Clara told them. "Then, the most incredible thing happened. You two better sit down. Do I have a story to tell you!"

Clara talked nonstop about the cardinal and Frank. Florence's mouth was still gaped open when she finished. Mary laughed until tears ran down her face. "Old Frank came through for you."

Chapter Thirty-Five

Disappointing News Threatens the Living Arrangements

ROBERT, JEAN, BRET, AND Sara arrived at Mary's a little before noon. Darcy was scheduled to arrive later in the day; she'd be coming straight from work, or so they all thought.

Clara hurried to the door on the second knock, smiling from ear to ear, excitement traveling through her body like a live electrical wire. Throwing the door open, she stood paralyzed in place—she couldn't decide who to grab and kiss first.

Sara came running into Clara's open arms, solving her problem. Within moments they were both equally engulfed in a warm embrace.

Bret followed suit. "Hello, Bret!" Clara cried. "Oh my, how you have grown since I saw you last. What are your parents feeding you, Grow Pup?" Bret smiled. He stood as tall as he could. Clara made no attempt to contain her happiness over seeing them all. She laughed and talked nonstop.

"We have a birthday present for you, Grandma!" Sara blurted out. Then she covered her mouth with both hands. Bret gave her a short rap on the head. "Ouch! That hurt," she exclaimed.

"Well, keep quiet then."

Clara covered up for Sara the best she could, trying to pretend she hadn't heard Sara spill the beans. She changed the subject, announcing that she had a gift for Bret and Sara that she wouldn't give to them until the party.

Just then Mary came into the hall and the hugs and kisses began again. Once she'd hugged her way through all her guests, she called out to Florence, who was still in the kitchen, to come and join them in the living room.

Everyone poured into the living room and settled in, the adults on chairs or the sofa, the children automatically making themselves at home by sprawling out on the floor. Everyone was quickly talking to somebody.

Florence finally joined them; she had wanted to give everyone a chance to say their hellos. She stood in the doorway, enjoying everyone's laughter and excited chatter. Mary got up, took her by the hand, and introduced her to each of them. Florence blushed when Robert and Jean each stood and hugged her. She was overcome with emotion at being so warmly accepted by Clara's family. Her shyness faded and before long she felt relaxed being in their company, as if she had known them all before.

∞

After lunch, Jean helped Mary clean up, then sat at the kitchen table with her while the others played a game of checkers at the big, round mahogany table in front of the living room window. Bret sat next to Florence and helped her. She proclaimed that she hadn't played checkers in over thirty years.

Outside the wind began to pick up and a few clouds played hide and seek with the sun. "How about a cup of tea, Jean?" Mary asked. They were both enjoying the peace and quiet. Finally, Jean broke the silence.

"How do you think Clara is doing, Mary? I mean, really doing? Robert is planning to talk with you in private, but he wants to wait until tomorrow, after the party."

Mary took in a long, deep breath. Her shoulders raised up slowly and then gradually relaxed. "What can I say?" she started. "I'm just so happy for her. She's doing so well. She's completely over that obsession with the dolls. She's eating well, and in my opinion she's happier than I've seen her in years. It's nothing short of a blessing to see her so happy."

Jean listened to Mary's story of how and where they found Florence, and could hardly believe it. "It was a miracle," was all she could say at the end.

"Florence's son agreed to let her stay with us through the weekend," Mary continued, "but he told me the other day that he's found a home for her here in South Port. What I think he'd really like to do, though, is take her back to Florida with him. But don't say a word, okay? Florence doesn't know. I begged him not to tell her until after this weekend. She's so happy here. I didn't want to spoil her fun."

All Jean could say was how sorry for her she was. It was going to be devastating to Florence to have to say goodbye to Clara. They had become such good friends.

The conversation drifted from Clara to Darcy. "I wonder where she is?" Mary said. "She should have been here hours ago."

It didn't surprise Mary that Darcy was late. It was a trait of hers that Mary was used to. But Mary had a strange feeling that Darcy was up to something, and whatever it was Mary was certain it would cause an explosion. She just hoped and prayed it wouldn't spoil the party. She didn't want it to ruin Clara's fun.

"Well, I know Robert and Darcy wanted to talk with you about Clara. About her going back home. But maybe I shouldn't..." Jean hesitated.

"What do you mean?"

"No one wants to take any further advantage of you."

"Take advantage of me!" Mary snorted. "That's utter nonsense. Clara's like a sister to me." Mary told her that she enjoyed Clara being there, and that it was good for her too. "I hadn't realized how lonely I was getting living here in this big, old house by myself." She smiled at Jean. "Having a meeting is a good idea. There are some things I want to discuss, too." Mary stopped and smiled. "I've known Robert and Darcy since they were babies. I practically raised Darcy." Now it was Jean's turn to smile. "Clara and Florence usually go to bed with the birds, so why don't we talk tonight after the party," Mary suggested tactfully.

"No, Mary, we don't want to spoil your day. After all, it's your birthday, too."

"Personally, dear, I'd prefer not to count the years anymore. I'm really doing this party thing for Clara. She's been through so much. I started planning this shindig with her in mind, not me."

∞

Darcy finally arrived, just as the table was being set. Mary was out in the kitchen, putting the finishing touches on the dinner and humming out loud as she so often did when she was happy. She could hear all the excitement and laughter of Darcy's arrival from the kitchen. She smiled to herself, happy that she and Clara's family could all be together. Having the party at her house was one of her best ideas in ages.

Darcy came running into the kitchen and hugged Mary. They rocked from side to side as they held each other.

Then Darcy held Mary at arm's length. Looking serious, she said, "Mary, I can't wait to tell Robert and Jean, but the reason I was late arriving is that I had an appointment with one of the social workers at Wood Lawn Nursing Home on my way over here."

Mary's smile disappeared. "Why would you want to do that, dear?" she asked Darcy, truly bewildered.

"Well, I don't know if you know it or not, but they always have an impossibly long waiting list. But I know someone who knows someone and, well, I'm pretty sure that we can get Mom in there! It's one of the best and most expensive places within ten miles of here. They have a swimming pool and big, clean, luxurious rooms, and you should see the lobby. It is to die for! They even have a floor-to-ceiling stone fireplace in the lobby and—"

Mary had to cut her short. "Now wait a minute, Darcy," she said suspiciously. "Does Robert know about this?"

"Not yet," Darcy admitted. "I was going to tell him, but I wanted to wait until I had a chance to talk to someone at the nursing home first," she said with a hint of agitation in her voice. "I didn't want to get everyone excited for nothing," she explained patiently. Then she looked more closely at Mary. "What's the matter, sweetie? You look like you've just seen a ghost."

"Well, dear," Mary said slowly, gathering her scattered thoughts. Darcy had really thrown her an unexpected curve ball. "I know you mean well, but I don't think Clara's going to be all that excited about it."

"Oh, she will be, once she sees the place," Darcy tried to assure her. "Anyone would be. It's a fabulous place."

"Yes, and I bet it has a fabulous price tag on it," Mary said dryly.

"Well, I don't know exactly what Mom's financial situation is. Robert takes care of that stuff, but I'm sure when the house is sold, it will cover her rent and then some."

"Don't you think you should have talked to Robert first, before you went and got yourself all excited about it?" Mary asked her.

"It'll be fine, Mary," Darcy promised her. "Don't worry. I know it will be just fine. I can handle Robert."

Mary was not happy; far from it. In fact, she was angry with Darcy, but she didn't want her dissatisfaction to show. Now was not the time. Their birthday celebration was about to begin and nothing was going to spoil that. She and Clara had waited a long time and had worked way too hard to make their birthdays special.

Chapter Thirty-Six

The Birthday Party

EVERYONE WAS SEATED COMFORTABLY around the table. Mary enjoyed using her finest tableware. The white linen tablecloth was her mother's best, and was still in perfect condition. She and Clara had polished the silver days before, and every piece of crystal and china was sparkling. Between two slender pewter candle holders holding tall white candles sat a glass bowl filled with exotic stones that held a bouquet of red and white short-stem roses.

The guests of honor, Clara and Mary, sat at either end of the table. Conversation was light and humorous, everyone taking turns telling a funny story of long ago. It was hard to hear the soft music of Nat King Cole singing "Mona Lisa" in the background.

The meal turned out even better than Mary had hoped for, and the adults savored a glass of red wine with their meal. While Bret and Sara enjoyed hearing the family stories, they could hardly contain themselves in anticipation of the birthday present surprise that they had for their grandmother and Mary. And there was Clara's surprise present from them, and the birthday cake that Mary made, just waiting to be eaten.

The afternoon wore on, and finally, before the cake was brought out, Clara excused herself, went and got the dolls and Teddy, and presented them to Bret and Sara with pleasure. They both thought their gifts were "cool," especially when they learned that they had once belonged to their dad and Aunt Darcy when they were young. Sara loved the dolls, and Bret, although a little too old for stuffed animals, would keep the teddy bear as a special souvenir from his grandmother. Clara whispered to him later that Teddy was her favorite.

Robert and Darcy looked at each other. Neither one needed to speak. They had just witnessed their mother letting go of a past illness that could not make an invalid of her anymore. The family in the attic was gone, replaced by real people. Darcy quickly wiped tears from her eyes with the back of her hand.

"Come help me in the kitchen," Jean told Sara. A few minutes later, they appeared at the door of the dining room, with Jean carefully carrying a birthday cake decorated with two intersecting circles of burning candles.

"One for Grandma and one for Mary," Sara explained as Jean set the cake before her grandmother. Mary came to the end of the table where Clara sat. The two old friends looked at each other, winked, held hands, and blew out all the candles.

Almost everyone was finished with their cake and ice cream when Sara, her cheeks full of cake, set to work getting her father's attention, wordlessly motioning to him, both hands flying in the air. Finally, Robert noticed. "Go!" he said, smiling, and without further ado, Sara jumped up and left the room, followed by Bret. "Mary, why don't you switch chairs with me so you can sit by Mom," Robert suggested.

Then Bret and Sara returned moments later with two tremendous, beautifully wrapped boxes, each with a huge green silk ribbon on top. Sara presented hers to Clara, and Bret gave his to Mary.

"Oh my goodness," gasped Clara. "These are just too pretty to open!"

"I agree," said Mary. "Maybe we should just leave them wrapped and display them on the side table."

"No!" Sara and Bret shouted in unison.

"Okay, okay," Mary grinned. "We'll open them."

Both women turned sideways in their chairs and set to work unwrapping each present. Once the bows were untied and the paper was taken off, their hands moved quicker. Matching tops came off matching boxes, only to reveal another pair of boxes inside them!

Clara and Mary stopped and looked up at each other, beaming like kids at their thirteenth birthday party. All eyes were on them. Florence was clapping and smiling and practically falling off her chair, straining to see what she could from where she was sitting.

"Florence, why don't you go stand over there," Jean suggested. "You'll be able to see better." Florence slowly pushed her chair back and, using both arms of the chair, stood up and walked over to get a better look.

The second pair of boxes revealed a third pair; the third, a fourth. After the fifth box had been opened only to find yet another, both Mary and Clara began to wonder if it was all just a joke. Finally, they came to a pair of tiny boxes about the size for a pair of earrings. Inside they each found a neatly folded piece of light blue parchment paper.

Mary got hers opened first. Turning to the group, she read it aloud. "This entitles you to one round-trip ticket to Bella Island, Mexico, and a seven-day, all-inclusive stay at the Marion Resort!" Her voice grew more excited with every word. Clara had followed along reading from her own copy, mouthing the words. Clearly, the two were identical.

Clara and Mary looked at each other, mouths wide open, incredulous and frozen in place. Everyone stood and gave the two stunned women a loud round of applause. Bret and Robert chimed in with ear-piercing whistles. Then Robert yelled, "Speech, speech!"

Mary turned to Clara. "You first, Clara. You're the oldest."

"And you never let me forget it," Clara started, then stopped as tears welled up in her eyes. Jean handed her a tissue. Taking in one quick breath, Clara placed her hand over her mouth, released it, and began.

"I am speechless," she grinned, "and overwhelmed with gratitude and happiness. What a wonderful surprise and way too generous. I can't thank you all enough for this. I know that we'll have the time of our lives. For those of you who don't know, the Marion Resort is where Frank and I had our honeymoon, over forty years ago." Everyone smiled and clapped; other than Florence, they did know.

When the clapping stopped, Mary stood tall, shoulders erect, head held high, and dark-brown eyes sweeping the table. She looked like a dignitary accustomed to making elegant speeches in front of large audiences. "All I can say is that you are all the most wonderful people I have ever known. God bless you all, and from the bottom of my heart, I do thank you. Clara has already said it, but I'll say it again: your gift is way too generous." She stopped, paused, and turned entirely serious. "There's only one problem with this kind gift."

She paused again and looked around the table. Everyone's smile had frozen in place. Stunned, no one spoke. Silence filled the air like helium fills a hot air balloon. Finally, Mary continued, her look even more serious. "Bella Island better get itself ready for us two red-hot mamas!" Everyone roared with laughter.

Florence attempted to make herself heard over everyone's laughter. "I have a speech," she tried to say. Bret, sitting next to her, was the only one who could hear her. He knew what was needed. "Shut up, everyone! Florence wants to talk!" he yelled at the top of his high-pitched soprano voice.

Everyone stopped and looked at Florence, who was now standing at her place at the table. "Thank you, Bret," she said with exaggerated politeness as she patted the top of his head. Bret winced. "What I want to say is that I have never been to a nicer birthday party in my life, and I've been to my share! For that, I thank you, Mary and Clara, for inviting me. I also want to thank the two of you again for rescuing me from the cold. Who knows, I could have ended up frozen to death. I keep wondering how they would have been able to get my dentures out of my head." Everyone chuckled.

"But in all seriousness," Florence continued, "I wish I had something that I could give you for your birthdays, but I don't, so please take a rain check on that and accept my love. A very happy birthday and many, many more."

Robert said, "Here, here!" and they all raised their glasses in succession.

Chapter Thirty-Seven

A Family Divided, Whose Life is it Anyway?

As MARY HAD PREDICTED, Clara and Florence went to bed exhausted once the party was over, all the dishes washed and put away, and the house back in order. Florence claimed that she'd sleep like a baby from the one glass of wine that she'd had. Bret and Sara were happily settled, watching a movie in one of the upstairs bedrooms, while the rest were all gathered in the living room, mugs of coffee in hand.

Robert started the difficult conversation. "It seems a shame to start discussing something this serious when we've had such a wonderful party, Mary."

"I know, dear," Mary acknowledged, "but this is a perfect time to talk, while Clara is fast asleep. No sense in getting her all shook up on her birthday. I know that we're here to talk about her returning home, but before I tell you what I have on my mind, maybe we should hear what Darcy has on hers. She's already told me what she's been up to." Surprised, Robert looked to Jean with a quizzical expression. She shrugged. She had no more idea what Mary was referring to than he did.

Darcy, who'd been lounging comfortably, sat up straight. Robert noticed she was chewing gum—historically, never a good sign with his sister. Something had her nervous.

"I have a friend," Darcy started, her voice pumped with an enthusiasm that to Robert's ear already sounded like a sales job, "who knows someone in management at a nursing home, right here in South Port, fifteen minutes from here or less. I don't know if anyone is aware of it or not, but it's very difficult—almost impossible—to get in there. They always have a waiting list. Anyway, I had an appointment to talk with the social worker there today. I saw her on my way here." She paused to let this much sink in. When no one commented, she continued.

"She gave me a tour of the place. I couldn't believe how fabulous it is." Caught up in her own agenda, Darcy failed to read the disbelief on the faces about her. She noticed Robert frowning, but had confidence she could turn his frown into a smile once he'd heard more. Obviously, he didn't know the place to which Darcy was referring.

She started ticking off its attributes on the fingers of her hand. "They have a swimming pool, and not just any swimming pool either, it's an Olympic-size one. In the lobby, the floor-to-ceiling fireplace is positively awesome. The rooms are large, with lots of light and huge walk-in closets, and they're all private. Each one even has its own bathroom. I didn't see any of the residents while I was there. They must have been in their rooms, or maybe they were playing bingo or something. But my point is, no one has to hang around with someone unless they want to."

Stunned at the thought, Robert folded his arms and set his jaw, but he didn't interrupt; he wanted to hear this thing out. He couldn't believe that his sister would even consider such a thing for their mother. He found himself wondering if perhaps she had gone totally mad. Darcy licked her lips and, if anything, chewed her gum even more nervously. "I have a lot more information," she plowed on. "They gave me a whole folder of information, which goes into all the details, including the cost. There are several ways you can pay. It is pricey, but only the best for Mommy, right?"

When did she last refer to Mom as "Mommy"? Robert wondered, shaking his head, his eyes pinned to the floor.

"Well ..." Darcy said, looking from Robert to Jean to Mary and back. "What do you think?"

No one spoke. The room was still except for the old grandfather clock faithfully ticking away in the corner. *If clocks could talk,* Mary thought.

Finally, when no one would comment, Darcy was forced to start in again. "All she has to do is see it. Who wouldn't want to live there? It's a high-class place. We'd be damn lucky to get her in there. The woman I spoke to today has pretty much given me the okay. It still has to go before the board. This is a very organized place and—"

Robert finally sat up and cleared his throat. Darcy stopped her presentation.

"Darcy," he said, his voice slow and icy, surprisingly reminding himself that he sounded like his dad when he was angry about something. "I've heard all I want to hear about this fancy-dancy place of yours. I have to say, I'm really surprised that you'd even consider this sort of thing without us talking about it first."

"I thought that you'd be happy that I finally did some legwork for you," Darcy interjected, "and took some initiative in looking into things for Mom. I wanted to surprise you."

"Well, you sure did that," Robert said loudly, standing up and putting his hands on his hips. "Actually, I'm more than surprised, Darcy. I am downright—excuse the expression—pissed off."

"Why?" Darcy said, genuinely amazed. "Mom's going to need a place to stay. We both agreed that her going home would be difficult, maybe even impossible."

"That's right. We did talk about her needing some help, but I never imagined her in a nursing home, especially not one that houses hundreds of people, like some overstuffed chicken coop, all closed up in their rooms so they never see another living person. If we've learned anything from the past month it's that isolation, Darcy, is in no one's best interest. Socialization is."

Darcy started to speak, but Robert put up his hand and stopped her. "When the time comes—or *if* the time ever comes—for Mom to have to go into an institution, I would prefer *small, warm,* and *cozy.* Don't you see, Darcy? Mom would be lost in a place that big. I was thinking of getting her services in the home, like Meals on Wheels, a housekeeper, an aide to help with cooking and shopping. Mom would never want to go to a place like what you're describing. It doesn't fit her personality."

Darcy stood up to face her brother, mockingly copied his hands-on-hips stance, and practically shouted, "How do *you* know?"

"Wait a minute here," Mary said, standing up and positioning herself between the two, arms outstretched to keep them apart. Jean sat wide-eyed, glued in place as the argument unfolded. She knew enough not to get in the middle of it. It was between Robert and Darcy to resolve it themselves, but she'd never seen them so angry at each other.

Mary intervened and got both to quiet down and to discuss things without shouting. "Everyone's entitled to an opinion," she said. Both Robert and Darcy backed down and returned to their seats. Mary was left standing in the middle of the room.

"Do either of you have anything else that you want to say?" she asked sternly. No one spoke. Darcy was again crying quietly into her tissue. "Well, I do. Clara and I have had a good time here together over these past weeks and—"

"That's another thing," Darcy interrupted. "You've done way more than we ever intended you to have to do."

"Are you done now?" Mary asked mildly. "I'd like to finish."

"Sorry," Darcy muttered. Mary stared her down.

"Not only has Clara enjoyed living here with me," Mary continued, "but I've come to realize that I don't want to live alone anymore. Funny, it took all this hitting me on the head like a ton of bricks to make me come to my senses. Life is short and my time here is getting shorter by the minute. I want to enjoy life, and I don't want to do it alone anymore. I have this big house and by God it feels good to have these old walls hear talking and laughter again." Now Darcy was the one who looked puzzled.

"Let me get to the point," Mary said. "I've asked Clara if she would like to live here with me, and guess what she said ... ?" No one spoke, but Robert's frown had turned itself back into a smile. He had a pretty good idea where this was going, and he liked what he was hearing.

"She said yes," Mary announced triumphantly. "She was planning on telling you this weekend. She wanted to surprise you." Darcy, who had stopped crying, looked up at Mary with red, swollen eyes. "Well," Mary said, "what do you think of that?" All eyes turned on Darcy.

"I think it's nice of you, Mary," she said carefully, like she was treading on thin ice. "And I am glad Mom said yes ... but I still say she should go just to see the place."

"I have no problem with that, Darcy dear," Mary said, stifling her recent annoyance. "You're right. She should have choices."

"Mary," Robert said, turning his back on Darcy to face her, "I can't think of a better place for Mom than right here in this house, and that's my vote."

Upstairs, Clara was standing in her nightgown in the doorway of her room, the door slightly ajar behind her. She'd heard it all. With Robert's final word on the subject, she flung both arms in the air. "That's my boy. Give 'em hell, son," she whispered to herself while grinning like a Cheshire cat.

The next morning, while everyone else was still asleep, Clara sat at the table with Robert and Darcy having a cup of coffee. Clara told them of her plan to live with Mary. She never let on that she had overheard the entire conversation the night before.

Nor did she mention to them her disappointment that they hadn't included her in the meeting. Their intention not to spoil her birthday with serious business was thoughtful of them, but it still bothered her that no one felt she could handle it. She was old, but surely not frail. She knew the children were only trying to protect her and that they wanted what was best for her. Robert took over where Frank had left off. Clara had confidence her son would take care of her money matters. Frank had left her well cared for. He had always been very organized, and Robert took after him.

Darcy was just the opposite. She was a procrastinator, always putting important matters off until another time. So, when she stepped in and tried to help Clara, it was hard to stay angry with her.

"I know my living with Mary is the right decision, despite anything the two of you may feel. I couldn't live alone in the house anymore. I like living here with Mary. I am finally getting over your father's death, to be honest, and I want to start having a little fun."

"Mother," Robert said, "I think Darcy has something she wants to tell you."

"What is it, Darcy?" Clara asked innocently.

Darcy took a sip of her coffee and then told Clara about Wood Lawn. Clara sat and listened, scowling as Darcy knew she would, never letting on that she had heard it all before.

"It sounds lovely, dear, but I don't see myself living around a lot of people I don't know. I know you mean well, honey, but I am not ready for a nursing home."

"But, Mother, it's not like a nursing home. You should at least see it."

"Mother's made up her mind, Darcy," Robert stepped in. "She wants to live here with Mary, and I for one think it's a great idea."

"That's fine," Darcy said testily, "but I want Mother to at least go and see the place. If she still doesn't want to live there, I'll happily let this whole idea go."

"Darcy," Robert said through gritted teeth, "let it go *now*."

"No," Clara said. "Darcy may have a point. You have a deal," she told her daughter. "I'll at least go and see it, but if I don't like it, please, do let it go." Turning to Robert, she said, "There's no harm in my seeing it. I should look at all my options. I'll get dressed and we will go today."

Darcy suddenly glowed; she'd finally gotten her way. She knew her mother would love it once she saw it. Wood Lawn would sell itself.

Chapter Thirty-Eight

Decisions Made

DARCY AND CLARA ARRIVED on time for their appointment to tour the nursing home. Clara climbed out of the car and took Darcy's arm. As she walked up the path that led to the front entrance, her pace grew slower with each step. She could not believe the size of the sprawling, one-level brick building that, joined together, looked like a circus train.

The grounds were impeccable. The afternoon sun made the place look like a swanky country club. Clara looked down at her clothes. *I should be wearing a cocktail dress,* she thought. *I feel out of place before I even get in the joint.* Glancing over at Darcy, she could see how thrilled she was with her choice of residence for her mother. Clara smiled back at her, not letting on how out of place she felt.

The lobby was entirely devoid of people. "Where is everyone?" Clara wondered aloud. She looked around and saw high ceilings, chandeliers, plush carpeting, and brown leather couches like those found in a snooty club. Clara was stunned. "Look at all that fancy Chippendale furniture. The way it's decorated, the president's mother must live here! And you weren't kidding about the floor-to-ceiling stone fireplace—they must have quarried half the Grand Canyon to build that thing!"

Paula, a tall blonde in a well-tailored black pantsuit, gave them the tour. *She talks nonstop about all the important people who've lived here. Who gives a rat's ass?* Clara thought, then felt mildly guilty at her coarse language. Darcy, on the other hand, was drooling over Paula's Gucci pantsuit. All three walked down the long, narrow, empty hallways. They seemed to go on forever. Clara couldn't help wondering how any elderly person could get from one end to another without having a heart attack. Hall after hall of doors to the residents' rooms were closed. It was so quiet, it felt like a tomb to Clara.

Darcy and Clara were introduced to anyone who happened to pass by. Everyone was pleasant and hoped that they would see her again. *Fat chance of that,* Clara thought to herself.

Darcy was dazzled by all the glitter. Clara couldn't wait to get back to Mary's.

On the drive back home, Clara sat quietly in the front seat, her hands folded in her lap, while Darcy jabbered on about what a great place it was, going back over her list of all its so-called "charms."

"Well," she finally said, "What do you think, Mother? Isn't it wonderful? I know it's big and probably a bit overwhelming at first. You probably need some time to think about it."

"No, honey," Clara said, "I've made up my mind."

Darcy took in a deep breath, her eyes pinned to the road as she drove, hoping her mother would agree how elegant and inviting Wood Lawn was, hoping she would want to move in right away.

"Darcy," Clara began, "I'm glad I went to see the place. You were right. I do need to see all my options, and that certainly is a beautiful one. I'm also grateful that you're trying to make my life comfortable, and I love you for it. But, it's not me. I'd feel like a fish out of water. I couldn't live in a place like that."

Darcy took her mother's hand while still keeping her eyes on the road. "Okay, Mother, I hear you," she said. "I know it's pretty fancy. I just wanted you to have the best."

"I will have the best, honey, living right there with Mary on the same street that I've lived on most of my life."

Then Clara changed the subject a bit, and asked Darcy to try to get along with Robert. "He wants what's best for me, too. Our family has always been that way: no grudges. I've always said I would rather have someone I care about in my life than to stay angry at someone and not have them in my life. A family that's strengthened by love and respect for each other is one of the greatest gifts we can hope for. I am the matriarch of this family, and one of my jobs is to hold us together."

After a long silence, Darcy finally spoke. "Okay, Mom." Clara smiled and turned her head to look out of the window. The rain had slowed and sun was trying to poke its head through row after row of evergreen trees. Darcy couldn't see the tears that welled up in Clara's eyes. They were tears of joy; she had made a decision.

When she could, Clara turned back to her daughter, and asked if she would help her decide what to take from home to Mary's. She knew Darcy was better at decorating than she was, and she thought if Darcy got involved in the move, it would make her feel better. Mary had told Clara she'd clear out the bedroom Clara was staying in so she could have the things from her home that she wanted.

Clara chatted on about what she thought she'd take, like her bed, the bureau, the old rocker ...

"And how about your desk from the living room?" Darcy asked. Clara had hoped that engaging her in the decorating phase of the move would help get her past any lingering ideas about a nursing home. It seemed to be working.

"You're right, how could I forget my desk?" Clara said, not that she had. "And maybe you could help me decorate the room, with pictures, lamps, and window covering from our home," she went on. "And I think I'll take my collection of mugs. I'll see if Mary minds. You can never have enough mugs. We have a cup of tea every afternoon, and always before bed. I swear that a cup of chamomile makes me sleep better."

"I didn't know that you were having trouble sleeping, Mom."

"I am doing nicely with the tea. I have Mary to thank for that. It was her idea and it works like a charm. She knows so much about nutrition and what some people might call old-fashioned cures for what ails you. You know I don't like pills."

The car sped along as the two of them pursued how they would decorate Clara's bedroom. Before Darcy knew it, she'd completely forgotten about Wood Lawn.

∞

Back at Mary's house, Robert, Jean, and the children had gone to the mall, a perfect thing to do on a cloudy afternoon. Florence and Mary were in the kitchen drinking a cup of tea when Clara and Darcy came in.

Mary and Florence sat quietly at the kitchen table.

Mary was deep in thought, recalling the conversations she'd had with Darcy. She knew Darcy was only trying to do what she felt was best. Even though Darcy knew staying with Mary would be good for Clara, she'd expressed reservations about what would happen should Clara suddenly take a turn for the worse again. Darcy had argued that if Clara was in a structured facility like a nursing home, she'd have all the medical care she'd need in an emergency.

"She's fine now, Mary," Darcy had said, "but what if she gets sick again."

"We'll do what we've always done, call 911. Besides, Darcy, this is what your mother *wants*. I didn't push this idea on her."

Florence interrupted Mary's thoughts. "I just wanted to thank you again for allowing me to stay for the weekend. I had such a nice time. I can't remember when I've had this much fun!"

"You are very welcome, Florence. I'm glad you were able to stay."

Florence asked when her son was coming for her to take her home, and Mary realized it was time to tell her what she had kept from her during the party.

"He's flying in tomorrow," she said.

"I wish I didn't have to go home," Florence said quietly. "I like being here with you and Clara."

Mary took another sip of her tea, desperate to think of something else to talk about. She knew that discussing her leaving would only make Florence sad, and it made Mary sad too. Finally, Mary said, "Your son only wants what's best for you."

"Mary, could I stay here with you and Clara?" Florence finally blurted out. "I have money. I'd pay my way, and I could be a help around the house, too."

Mary sighed deeply, wishing she could say, "Sure, Florence, you can stay here." But she knew that Paul was on his way and he had already paid money to hold a place for her at an assisted care home. It was up to him to break the news to his mother, not her.

"Talk to Paul about it," she heard herself saying before she could stop the words from coming out of her mouth. "But Florence," she rushed to add, "I don't think you should get your hopes up. Paul may already have something else in mind."

"I know. I have an apartment, and he'll want me to stay until the end of the month because it's paid up until then. But after that, I'm sure he won't mind, especially once he meets you and sees your beautiful home."

"Florence," Mary interrupted, "we should just wait and talk about it more when he gets here."

"You're right," Florence agreed reluctantly. "We should wait." There was nothing she'd love to talk about more. "When did you say he would be here?"

"Tomorrow."

"I can wait one more day. You know, he's always been a good son," Florence mused. "I can't imagine what my life would've been like without him. He's kind, and smart too. Always was a good student in school. You know, Mary, all I ever think about is his finding the right woman someday and having a family. He'd make a good father, and husband. What I wouldn't give to have grandchildren like Clara. She's lucky, and she knows it." Florence was on a roll, clearly just warming up to her subject. "If he doesn't hurry up, he's going to be too old to have kids and I'll be dead in my grave. If you ask me, he travels way too much. No woman would put up with him, traveling all the time like he does. I'm old, you know. I'll be seventy-eight on my next birthday. I can't believe it. I don't feel seventy-eight. I can still touch my fingers to my toes. Watch this."

Florence stood up, took a deep breath, flung her chubby arms up over her head, then bent down to touch the tips of her toes. Her arms came up and she bent over for the second time and touched them again. When she tried to do the maneuver for the third time, Mary grabbed hold of her arm to stop her.

"Okay, Florence, that's enough!" she laughed. "You've convinced me you're in tiptop shape. Fact of the matter is, I don't feel my age either. I've exercised all my life. I've always felt better when I do. Eating right, exercise, and vitamins are what keep Dr. Hoyt away from me," Mary said with a wink. "Now, if we can keep Clara interested in taking chair yoga classes three times a week with us, we'll all stay gorgeous. No apple figures, no double-wide back ends, no bellies that connect with the boobs."

Chapter Thirty-Nine

Heartfelt Advice

DARCY DECIDED IT WAS the perfect time to tell her mother about her boyfriend. She had to tell her sooner or later anyway. She wanted her mother to meet him. She knew that once she did, she would see what a good person he was.

Once Clara and Darcy arrived back home, Darcy turned the car off while the two of them sat in silence for a few moments before going into Clara's house to begin collecting a few things they could easily carry back to Mary's. They would arrange for the rest of the furniture to come at another time.

Darcy sighed and found herself telling her mother all about Jeff.

What she had just heard from Darcy had come as a complete bolt from the blue. She wasn't sure how to respond.

Darcy could see that what she had just told her mother had shocked her, and knew that she would need a few moments to digest what she had just heard. She took the kettle from the stove, went to the sink to fill it, and put water on for tea. All the while, Clara sat stone-faced and speechless.

Darcy was starting to regret telling her mother about Jeff. *Why on earth did I think Mother could handle that sort of information?* She reached over and took Clara's hand. "Are you okay, Mother?" she asked gently.

Clara looked at her daughter and finally nodded. "I'm fine now, honey. I just needed a moment. Darcy," she said, taking a deep breath, "I think it's time I told you *my* secret."

Still holding her mother's hand, Darcy looked at her, puzzled. Her mother's face wore a more serious expression than she could ever remember seeing. Clara cleared her throat and began. "I bet you think your father is the only man I ever had in my life."

Before Darcy could answer, Clara continued. Just like Darcy, she also needed to get this off her chest. "I know I've been nagging you these past few years to settle down and get married. I did it because I wanted you to experience how it feels to love and to be loved in return. I loved your father, but not in the way I had hoped I might. My parents pushed me into marrying Frank. They didn't want a scandal. Small towns love scandals. The man I truly loved was Dave."

"Mother! I'm shocked!" Darcy said, covering her mouth with both hands. "I never imagined you ... who was Dave?"

"Just let me continue, Darcy. We'll get to 'who he was' in a minute. Dave and I met and dated all through high school. We were instantly attracted to one another. At first my parents thought it was harmless, but when they realized how serious I was getting, they forbade me to see him."

"Why would they do that, Mother?" Darcy interrupted, mystified. "Lots of people date in high school. You always let me date boys when I was in high school."

"We both knew the reason; it was because he was from mixed parents. His mother was white and his father was black. Because we weren't allowed to see each other, it forced us to date secretly. One night while we were out at 'Lover's Lane,' we went too far. I got pregnant." Clara waited for Darcy to absorb this much information before she continued. Finally, she pressed on.

"My parents forced me to carry the baby to term. They were good Catholics. I was sent away to live in a home for unwed mothers in New York until the baby was born. Then I returned home to finish my last year of school. The baby was placed for adoption. No one in town ever found out."

"What happened to Dave?" Darcy asked. "Did you ever hear from him, or see him again?" She looked as if she'd just been hit with a bolt of lightning.

"You asked who Dave was. He was your father's best man at our wedding."

Darcy's hand went to her mouth again. "Oh yes, now I remember you telling me about him," she said, more to herself than to her mother. "You said that he and Dad were best friends."

"That's right. After the wedding, he wrote and told me he would never try to contact me again. I knew he had joined the army, but that was all I ever heard."

Darcy could barely accept what she was hearing. She looked at her mother, but couldn't believe that this was the same person she had known all her life. She knew her mother was strong-willed, but this was more than she ever imagined her mother would do. She sat quietly, shaking her head while Clara finished pouring her heart out about Dave. Then her mother returned to Darcy's dilemma.

"Honey, if you love someone, you do what your heart tells you to do," she said. "But first, it seems to me this Jeff person has to get divorced. If he loves you, Darcy, he'll find a way. But please understand, I'm not going to interfere in your life. I'm glad you've finally found someone. Just please do the right thing and make him divorce her. You'll never be happy as long as he is married."

Darcy knew everything her mother said was right. She planned to see Jeff as soon as she got back home. Time was up. He had to divorce Stella. She had left several messages on his cell phone over the weekend, but so far, he hadn't returned any of them. She was beginning to wonder if Stella had told him about her call. If she had, he could be furious with her.

Darcy decided she didn't care. Either he ended his marriage or they were finished. In her heart she didn't want to believe Stella's lies about Jeff having other women. The thought of it was too difficult for her to even consider.

Chapter Forty

A Mug Portrays Feelings

EVERYONE SPENT A NICE evening together. The air had cleared between Darcy and Robert. Clara spent as much time with Bret and Sara as she could; she dreaded the next day when they all would have to leave.

Mary was glad to see that there were no more hard feelings between Robert and Darcy. She disliked arguments. But no family she ever heard of was without them. She also knew Clara well enough to know that Wood Lawn would never be a place Clara would like. On the other hand, she was glad Clara had pacified Darcy by going with her to see the nursing home.

Florence didn't discuss staying with Mary and Clara any more that evening, but the next day, once everyone had left to go home and it was just the three of them again, she brought it back up. They were having breakfast.

"When did you say my son was coming?" Florence asked for the tenth time since she'd heard the news.

"He'll be here within the hour, Florence," Mary told her once again.

"Good. I can't wait to see him," Florence said. "I know he'll go for the idea of my staying here with you two. It'll take a load off his mind, not having to worry about me living alone."

"Florence," Clara dared to ask before Mary could stop her, "what if he says no?"

"He won't," Florence said. "I know him well enough to know that all he wants is for me to be happy."

"Well, that's nice," Mary intervened. "I can't wait to meet him. You've talked so much about him; I feel like I already know him."

The morning flew by as all three chattered about what a wonderful party it had been. Clara and Mary were excited about the trip to Mexico they would be taking together. They talked about how much fun it was going to be.

After they had finished cleaning up from breakfast, they sat around the table talking up a blue streak. Clara and Florence reminisced about the good times they'd had taking trips with their husbands. Mary listened intently as they talked about this and that. Smiling at how happy they both were, she was happy, too.

"I haven't heard you talk about a man," Florence said to Mary. "You're an attractive woman. There must have been someone special in your life."

"You've never heard me talk about my man, as you put it, because I never married. I had one or two men in my life, but it never got to the point of marriage. The only man I truly loved was Moe."

Mary stopped and suddenly squeezed her eyes shut as if she was trying to keep from crying. Then she put her head down. The room was silent. It was clear to both Clara and Florence that she didn't want to talk about it. Clara knew what had happened and wasn't about to pursue the subject; she knew how difficult it was for Mary to talk about Moe. In fact, it had been years since the painful subject had last come up. But Florence pressed on, before Clara could stop her.

"What happened to him?" Florence asked.

Mary looked up at her, took a deep breath, and said quietly, "He was killed in an automobile accident. A week before we were to be married." Florence gasped. Sadness filled the air.

"I'm so sorry, Mary," Florence said. She reached over and tenderly touched Mary's hand. "You don't have to talk about it if you don't want to."

But Mary took another deep breath and continued. "It was a long time ago. I was only twenty-seven. He was twenty-nine. He was way too young to die.

"I can see him now as plain as day. Tall, thin. He always wore a baseball cap. I bet he had a dozen of them. The dimple on his chin made him look a little like Malcolm X. Moe and my mother could sit in our kitchen for hours, trying to outtalk one another. You could hear their belly laughs from everywhere in the house. I'd sit in the living room pouting, angry he wasn't sitting with me. My mother would shake her head when I complained and say, 'He likes having a good time, honey. You just better get used to it.'

"Moe and I had lots of talks about our future together. We both wanted to have children someday. It was important to him 'to leave his mark here on earth,' is how he put it. I had completed nursing school by then and was working. Poor Moe couldn't seem to figure out what he wanted to be. He never went to college, so he settled for menial jobs just making enough money to pay his rent. It didn't bother me, but my mother never liked it that he didn't have a college education. 'He'll find something someday,' I argued in his defense, but secretly I knew it might never happen.

"I tried not to let it bother me. I was in love with him, plain and simple. If we had a lovers' quarrel about something, we never stayed angry. He knew all he had to do was kiss me and I'd melt."

Mary looked from Florence to Clara, who both sat listening intently. Then Mary smiled and said, "Want to know a secret?" They both nodded in unison in anticipation of what they were about to hear. Mary spoke softly. "I heard bells ring every time he kissed me."

Clara and Florence leaned in a little closer. "You heard bells ring every time he kissed you?" Florence repeated.

"You heard it correctly," Mary replied, then said it again, this time loudly. "Every time he kissed me, I heard bells ring. I've thought about it and I think it happened so I would know him in our next life. Let's face it, hearing bells ring when someone kisses you just doesn't happen."

"You never told me that part before, Mary," Clara said, stunned.

"I have never told anyone about it. I was sure people would either think I'd gone mad or just not believe it. After all this time I can hardly believe it myself."

Mary turned to Florence. "You asked me how Moe died. I'll never forget that day. Moe had just rented an apartment. I was at his apartment, tidying things up a bit. I wanted him to be surprised when he came home from work. I had opened the windows to let in the fresh air.

"I was surprised when Moe came home early in the day. He'd been drinking. I could smell it. He told me he'd been laid off. He was depressed and decided to drown his sorrow in quite a few beers. I was disappointed in him for how he dealt with the situation.

"It wasn't the first time that had happened. Usually, I just left it alone. I didn't want to cause an argument. This time I let him know how upset I was. I let the door slam as I left the apartment and headed for home.

"About midnight I heard the phone ring. I was living with my parents until we were to be married. I heard my mother say something about the 'hospital.' Then she called me to the phone. It was about Moe. He'd been in a car accident and the ER nurse was calling me at his request.

"To this day I don't remember the drive to the hospital. But I will never forget the look on his face when he saw me. 'See what happens when you get mad at me?' he said. 'Please don't blame me,' I begged him. He looked so pitiful. He was in a lot of pain. And he was paralyzed. He'd broken his neck. He was lucky to be alive at all.

"The next day I went to my mother. I always went to her when I had a problem. 'Do you think he'll be okay?' I asked her with tears in my eyes.

"Then she said something I would expect of her. She said, 'Let's pray.' I went to her and knelt at her knees. I prayed harder than I had ever prayed in my life. When I was finished, I looked up at her. 'Now,' she said, 'pray again. This time you must ask the Lord that it be his will if Moe lives or dies.'

"I did as she asked. Suddenly an old wooden cross that was sitting on top of her dilapidated-from-use family bible fell off the table and onto the floor. We couldn't believe our eyes. I had been given my answer. Two days later I got a call from his sister telling me that due to complications from the accident, he'd had a massive stroke and was dead."

Mary wiped the tears from her eyes with the back of her hand. Clara got up, took the box of Kleenex, and passed it around to everyone. No one could speak until Mary finally said, "No more sad stories. Moe is at peace; God rest his soul. I have a lot to be thankful for. I've missed him, but I wouldn't trade my life for anything."

Chapter Forty-One

In the Mood for Love

THEY WERE STILL SITTING around the table, once again talking and laughing about the weekend, waiting for Paul to arrive, when they heard a knock at the door. "That's probably your son, Florence," Mary said as she headed for the front door.

Opening the door, Mary was surprised to find a postman standing there, tall and thin with wide, gold-rimmed glasses. With his salt-and-pepper hair, he looked a lot like Jimmy Stewart. "I was about to deliver a certified letter next door when a neighbor of yours said I would find Clara Lewis at this address," the postman said.

"Why, yes, she's here. Let me get her for you. Clara," Mary yelled from the hall, "the postman has a letter for you."

"A letter for me?" Clara said as she made her way to the door.

Mary stepped out of the way as Clara reached for the letter the postman held out to her. "It's certified, so if you'll sign right here, I'll be on my way." He handed her a clipboard.

Clara signed the receipt that was attached to the clipboard and handed it back to the postman. He turned and headed down the steps, then yelled as he was halfway back to his truck, "Good day, ladies."

Clara stood in the doorway, turning the letter over and over in her hand, stunned. Who would be sending her a certified letter? For some reason she suddenly felt weak; she had been struck by a ridiculous yet powerful premonition. Mary took Clara by the arm and led her back to the kitchen.

"Sit down, honey, and open it," Mary suggested.

The mysterious thing about the letter was that it had no return address. Clara started to tear open the envelope. Mary stopped her. "Wait a minute, dear. Let me get you a letter opener."

Mary came back from the living room with a long silver letter opener. Florence and Mary sat wide-eyed at the kitchen table holding their breath in anticipation.

Clara pulled a single piece of paper out of the envelope and let her eyes fly to the bottom of the page, anxious to see who had written it. Her mouth dropped open as she gasped at the name. It read, "Love, Dave." She was holding the letter in front of her with both hands, which were shaking as if she was in the midst of a sudden earthquake.

"What is it?" Mary asked. "What on God's green earth is the matter, Clara?"

Clara didn't answer. She was speechless. When Mary saw her eyes swell with tears, she quickly pushed her chair back from the table and came around to place both her hands on Clara's shoulders, which were shaking as well.

"I ... I'm alright," Clara said. "I just need a little time alone. Would you mind if I went to my room for a minute?" She reached around and placed one hand on top of Mary's.

"Are you sure you'll be alright?" Mary asked.

"Yes, really, Mary. I just need a moment alone." Clara folded the letter and placed it back in the envelope, wanting to read it in private, and anxious to find out why after all these years Dave would be writing her.

He was alive! She hadn't heard from him since the war. Now, after all these years, he was contacting her. Why?

Mary stood in the kitchen door watching as Clara climbed the stairs, her head bowed, holding onto the railing as she slowly took one step at a time—as if she knew she was about to open up Pandora's box. She knew her myths. Pandora had set free Greed, Vanity, Slander, Envy—and Pining. She'd slammed the lid shut, leaving only Hope within.

"Well, what was all that about?" Florence asked.

Mary turned back to face her. "Poor thing. I hope it isn't bad news. I'm sure she'll let us know what it's all about in due time. In the meantime, we'll just give her space. She's made it clear she needs time alone."

Well, this day certainly is starting out with a bang, Mary thought to herself. *First Clara gets a mystery letter, and any minute now, when Paul arrives, Florence is going to get the bad news about having to go into an assisted care home.*

No sooner had the words formed in her mind than there was another knock at the front door. "Oh dear, here we go," Mary said aloud as she went to open it.

On the step was a tall, thin, handsome man who looked to be in his late forties. His black mustache followed the contours of a wide smile. "Hi. I'm Paul Foster, Florence's son," he said by way of introduction. "I'm looking for Mary."

"I'm Mary. Won't you come in," she said pleasantly, looking for—and finding—a suggestion of surprise at discovering that his mother had just spent the weekend with a total stranger, and a black one at that. "Your mother's in the kitchen having coffee. Won't you join us?"

"Thanks. I could use a cup. It's been a long flight." He stepped into the foyer, glancing around at the various rooms. He appreciated fine detail and quality architecture. The beautiful crown moldings, high ceilings, and hardwood floors caught his eye instantly. "Nice home you have here, Mary," he said as he followed her into the kitchen.

Florence jumped to her feet at the sound of her son's voice. Within seconds they were both locked in a warm embrace. "It's so good to see you, son," she exclaimed.

"It's good to see you, too, Mom. I've missed you."

"Mary this is my son, Paul. Paul, this is Mary," Florence said proudly.

"Yes, we met at the door," Paul told her, but both shook hands again to appease Florence. "I can't thank you enough for finding my mother and then for letting her stay here for the weekend on top of that," he told Mary. "You have my greatest thanks."

"Your mother is a delight," Mary responded as she poured him a cup of freshly made coffee. "It's been my pleasure."

"I understand that you have another friend staying here, too?" Paul went on. "Clara's the name, if I remember correctly."

"Yes, she's upstairs. You'll meet her later," said Mary.

"She got a letter today," Florence added, "And she wants to read it alone."

"Oh, I hope it's good news," Paul said.

Florence ignored his remark. She had her own agenda. "Son," she said warmly, leaning over closer to get a better look at him and taking his hand. "I have something I need to tell you." And before Paul could say another word, she launched into a lengthy and detailed narrative about the party and about how she loved being with Clara and Mary.

Paul finally put up his hand and tried to cut in and stop her in mid-sentence, but Florence kept right on talking. "Anyway, son, I've decided I am not going back to the apartment. I am staying right here with Clara and Mary."

"No, Mother, that's not going to happen," Paul said as gently as he could.

"What do you mean?" Florence sputtered. "Mary said she'd love to have me, didn't you, Mary?"

"Yes, Paul, that's right," Mary said. "I would like for her to stay here if it's okay with you. Clara and I are going to live here together and one more person would be even more fun. Really, Paul, I would very much like to have her."

"Mary, I thank you for the offer, but like I told you on the phone, I have made other arrangements for Mother."

"What arrangements?" Florence cried out.

"They're holding a nice room for you at Gretchen's Place, an assisted care home here in South Port."

"No!" Florence said angrily, "I am not going to any nursing home, not now, not ever. How dare you try to force something like that on me? I'm not going, and furthermore, Paul, you can't make me go."

"Mother, please listen to reason," Paul said. "May I remind you that you walked away from the daycare center last week and got lost. I'm living in Florida, Mother. I can't be available to you."

"Well, I don't need you to be available to me," Florence retorted. "I can take care of myself."

"Mother, listen," Paul said, a little more firmly. "This isn't the first time that you've gotten lost. Remember a few months ago when you got lost and the police found you wandering around in the park and had to bring you back home?"

"Well, that was different," Florence huffed.

"What was different about it?" Paul asked her, exasperated. "Lost is lost."

"I wasn't lost. I was just sitting in the park enjoying the scenery."

"Then why were you crying when the police officer found you?"

"Well," Florence lied, "it just so happens that those were tears of joy."

"Mother," Paul pressed on, "I know this is hard for you, but I've let you talk me out of a safer living situation long enough. I can't let you live alone anymore, and living here is out of the question."

Mary looked from one to the other, then covered her face with her hands. They were talking back and forth and getting nowhere. She could understand Paul not wanting his mother to live with a total stranger. "I am going to let you two work this out alone," she said. She got up and headed for the stairs, wanting to check on Clara anyway.

"Wait a minute, Mary," Florence pleaded. "Please tell Paul that he can't do this."

"Florence, I can't get involved," Mary said as kindly as she could. "This is between the two of you. I have already said that you are entirely welcome here."

Mary headed for the stairs. She could hear the two of them talking over one another, neither one listening to the other. One of them would be the winner, the other the loser. Mary could only pray that whatever happened would be for the best.

Mary knocked lightly on Clara's bedroom door. "Can I come in?" she asked.

"Yes, come in, Mary," Clara answered.

She found Clara sitting on the bed, the letter still in her hand. Her face was red and her eyes were puffy from crying.

Mary sat down on the bed beside her and put her arm around her shoulder. "Want to talk about it, honey? It might make you feel better if you got whatever it is out in the open."

Mary knew that if she could get Clara to talk, it would be a small miracle. Neither spoke. Knowing that sometimes silence is best, Mary didn't say a word. She just waited.

Finally, Clara said, "okay, Mary, I think it's time to come clean."

Both of them took in a deep breath at the same time: Mary's a sigh of relief, Clara's because she was letting go of a long-kept secret that was both painful and frightening. "The letter is from Dave," Clara said. "You remember Dave, Frank's best man at our wedding?"

"Yes, I remember him," Mary said, puzzled, "But I thought he was either dead or missing from the war. That's what you told me, not all that long ago."

"I know. But he isn't. He's alive and well. He ... wrote me."

"Why would he be writing you after all these years?" Mary asked.

"Maybe it would be better if you just read the letter. It explains some of it," Clara said as she handed the letter over to Mary.

Mary began to read it, first slowly and then more quickly, with a look of complete shock and surprise.

Dear Clara,

I hope this letter finds you well. I had to write you, Clara. I dreamt of you last night, as I have many times before. I know hearing from me now comes as a shock, but I want to let you know I'm living in a retirement home in California.

It would take a book to explain my life to you after all these years, and all I have been through, good and bad. So, I'll just keep it brief for now in the hopes that we can both fill in the gaps someday over a cup of coffee. I want to say how sorry I am to hear about Frank. I wanted to write or send flowers or something when he passed away, but I knew you were going through a difficult time and I didn't want to compound it with the shock of hearing from me. I've been receiving the local South Port paper for years; that's how I knew about his death.

I never wrote to you after the war because I was in pretty rough shape for a long time. I was in a prisoner of war camp for almost eight months. It took me years to get over the pain and suffering caused by the war.

By then, what was the point of writing? You were married and raising a family, so I decided to never interfere in your life again. I only wanted what was best for you. I am sorry for any pain my not telling you I was alive may have caused you. I wrote you right after your wedding. That was the last time you heard from me. I wanted it to be that way for both our sakes.

My wife of thirty years passed away two years ago; I am widowed, too. Time heals wounds, Clara. I know your loss will heal in time, too. It would be wonderful to be in touch with you again. I'll wait for your reply. You can reach me by using my forwarding address on the letterhead.

Love,
Dave

Mary placed the letter in her lap and turned to look at Clara. There were tears in her eyes now. "My goodness, Clara. I never knew that you had those kinds of feelings for Dave and he towards you."

"The amazing thing is that I told Darcy about him just the other day. And now his letter. Mary,"

Clara said quietly, looking up at her friend. "I never stopped loving Dave."

Mary smiled. "Well, alright then, girl," she said. "You go for it! Write him back!"

Clara admitted that she couldn't love Frank after the depression had set in, the way she had before. She'd stayed with him for the children's sake. Now it was her time. She would seize the moment, she declared, and begin corresponding with Dave.

"Mary, this is one of the happiest moments of my life," she announced. "You know what? Life doesn't begin at forty. I think it can begin at any time. For me, life is beginning again right now."

Both women smiled and embraced. Mary was happy for Clara. She was also happy for herself.

Chapter Forty-Two

A Haunting Secret from the Past Comes to Light

CLARA PULLED HERSELF TOGETHER and came downstairs with Mary, eager to meet Florence's son. She found the two of them still in a discussion over Florence going to an assisted care home.

It was clear that Paul was frustrated over not getting his mother to understand, but he was standing his ground. His mother was going to an assisted care home and that was that. He was not going to go back to Florida to worry himself sick over her anymore. She needed to be in a safe place, and if she didn't want to move to Florida and let him be part of her life, what could be safer than an assisted care home?

Mary and Clara sat down at the table and immediately felt like they were in the stands watching a tennis match as they followed the quarrel back and forth. The two only stopped arguing long enough for Mary to introduce Paul to Clara, then they picked up where they'd left off.

Finding him most attractive, Clara immediately found herself wishing there was some way she could introduce Paul to Darcy. She already knew from Florence that he was eligible, a nice guy, and wealthy to boot. *There you go again, Miss Matchmaker,* she laughed at herself. She couldn't help it; it seemed to be a reflex with her.

Suddenly Mary knew what it was she had to say. "Florence," she interrupted, "I know you don't want to go to a nursing home, but you have to try to understand. Your son is worried about you being alone in your apartment. He's a smart man, and a good son. He has found a place for you to stay that's licensed, and the way Paul has described the place it sounds like a nice place. It's much smaller than a nursing home. It is called an assisted care home. They have caregivers around the clock. You won't be lonely. Now, you don't want to worry him anymore do you, dear? Staying with Clara and me is not an option. But what if we came and got you and took you out once in a while? That way you could spend time with us."

Florence fiddled with her hands, twisting them around and around, not responding. Instead, she looked around the table. All eyes were staring at her. Everyone was holding their breath. "Okay," she finally said. "I don't want to fight about this anymore. I'm tired."

"So, you'll go?" Paul asked.

"Yes, but only because I'll still get to see my friends. I never want to lose my friends."

"Florence, was that what you were worried about?" Mary asked. "You were afraid you wouldn't see us again?" Florence nodded. "You'll never lose our friendship, dear. Please believe that," Mary said.

Clara smiled and took Florence by the hand and gently squeezed it. "We're friends for life," she added.

Paul couldn't thank Mary enough. Once again, Mary, a total stranger, had helped him out. "If there is ever anything I can do for you, Mary, please just let me know. I owe you so much," he told her.

Standing at the door, suitcase in hand, Florence turned to Clara and hugged her. "I love you, Clara," she said. "Promise you'll come and see me soon."

"I'll come tomorrow, Florence," Clara assured her as she kissed Florence's cheek, moist with tears.

Mary hugged her, too, and whispered in her ear at the same time. "Be strong, Florence," she said. "You can do it." Florence looked from Mary to Clara, then blew them a kiss, and winked. Paul grabbed her suitcase, Florence latched onto his free arm, and the two of them left. Mary and Clara stood in the doorway, waving goodbye until they drove off.

Mary and Clara retreated to the kitchen, both feeling sad at having to see Florence leave. Mary finally broke the silence. "Okay, Clara, we can't sit around at the table all day feeling blue like this. It's been quite a morning. First that unexpected letter from Dave and then Florence leaving. I don't think I can take any more excitement. I've had enough for one day. More than enough!"

"Me, too," Clara had to agree.

"So, my dear, what are you going to do about Dave?"

"l don't know yet. I want to think about it."

Mary put down her cup and looked at Clara. "You're still in shock over getting his letter, aren't you?"

Clara nodded, then took a deep breath and slowly exhaled. "I want to see him, Mary, but I'm scared to death."

"Scared of what?" Mary probed.

"My feelings for him, I guess," Clara replied, tentatively, testing the idea out loud. "Come on, Mary. Let's go into the living room and get comfortable. I have a long story to tell you about Dave and me. I haven't told you everything."

The two woman sat facing each other, Clara seated comfortably on an overstuffed chair, one leg crossed over the other, Mary on the matching couch. Clara inhaled deeply, then relaxed, audibly letting air out through her pursed lips. The room was quiet. Mary could tell Clara was grappling for a way to begin.

"Dave and I had an affair in high school," she finally said. "We were in love. Of course, my parents forbade me to date him. He wasn't 'good enough' for me. They wanted me to marry a good Irish boy. No way would they stand for me having anything more than a platonic friendship with Dave."

"I can imagine," Mary empathized. "That just wasn't 'done' in those days."

"So, we were crafty about finding ways to be together. In the beginning it was just a little petting, but then one night at 'Lover's Lane' after a football game, it happened. We just couldn't help ourselves. We were so in love." Clara stopped, then forced herself to say the fateful words. "I got pregnant, Mary. There was a child."

Mary gasped, then pressed her hands to her mouth, hardly believing her ears. A tear rolled down Clara's cheek. Mary fumbled for the Kleenex box on a table by the couch and handed it to her. For a moment, neither spoke.

Clara sighed, then continued. "My father screamed at me. I thought he was going to kill me. He told me I was lucky he didn't disown me, that I had disgraced the family. My parents and I were sitting at the kitchen table. I'll never forget it. My mother and I were both crying. I had my head on the table. I couldn't look either of them in the eye.

"It was the first time I ever heard my mother stand up to my father, and I remember every word as if it was just yesterday. My mother told him to leave me alone. She said, 'Can't you see how upset she is? Do you want to give her a heart attack, and me one too?'

"I don't think I'd ever seen my father looking as furious as he did at that moment. Then my mother simply said, 'Calm down honey and try to talk without yelling,' real quiet-like. I lifted my head from the table and looked at my father. He turned his face away from me. I can still see the look of disgust on his face.

"It was my mother who talked my father into at least letting me carry my child to term and then putting it up for adoption. I had no other choice. Of course, Dave wanted us to get married, but I knew my parents would never let that happen. We were never alone again. Dave came home only for short visits from college, but we never saw each other.

"What we did changed our lives. I didn't speak with him again until he came home for the wedding. He was Frank's best man, as you know."

"My goodness, Clara, I never suspected," Mary said, shaking her head. "How did you carry a child without anyone ever knowing?"

"It was easy in the beginning; it didn't show much. I was skinny as a rail in those days. I wore baggy clothes to conceal my growing stomach. I was about seven months along when my mother sent me to a home for unwed mothers. I had the baby there. A boy. I returned to school just in time to graduate with the class. I tried to get my mother to let me keep the baby, but she wouldn't hear of it."

"That had to have been so hard—giving up a child," Mary said.

"I thought of him—my boy—for years. I still do," Clara admitted. "I wondered what he looked like, where he lived, and what sort of person he turned out to be. I've paid for my mistake every day of my life."

Mary just couldn't stop shaking her head. "How unnatural. How cruel," she murmured.

"Dave wrote to me after Frank and I got married. We both knew we had to forget the past and move on with our lives. But you know something, Mary?"

"What's that, Clara?"

"We never stopped loving each other."

Mary stood up and started pacing, trying to comprehend all that Clara had told her. "What a story, Clara. It must have been so hard for you, not having anyone you could talk to about it."

"I had to keep the secret, and I was so ashamed. I couldn't even tell you. So many people have been hurt," Clara explained.

Mary took Clara's hands in hers. "I'm so sorry, honey. What a dreadful thing to have to go through."

"I wanted to tell you so many times, Mary, but I couldn't," Clara said sadly. "I hope you'll forgive me. What are best friends for if you can't tell them everything?"

"I understand, dear, and besides, you're telling me now, aren't you?" Mary responded warmly.

"I want to see Dave," Clara said, almost to herself. "We have so much to talk about."

Mary watched the creases on Clara's forehead deepen. "What is it, honey? Is there more?"

Clara's lips had compressed into a thin line; words were stuck deep in her throat, as thick as cold honey. The conversation had ended. Clara had told Mary all she could. She neither wanted to, nor was able to, talk about it anymore.

Chapter Forty-Three

Gretchen's Place

THE NEXT MORNING, MARY and Clara were sitting at the kitchen table having coffee. Clara's mug read, "Happiness Is Doing What You Love." Mary's read, "God Bless This Home."

Suddenly there was a knock at the front door. "I'll get it, Mary," Clara said. "You relax and have your coffee." Clara opened the door and couldn't believe her eyes. Standing at the door, suitcase in hand, was Florence.

"Florence!" Clara cried, "What in the world are you doing here? And how did you get here?"

"Oh, just relax," Florence said breezily, as she waved the cab driver away. "There was no way I was going to stay at that home. I just went along with it until I could get Paul out of town. It was a nice place and all, but not for me."

Mary stepped into the hall. At the sight of Florence and her suitcase, her eyes grew to the size of malt balls. "Florence, what on earth ...?" She couldn't even finish her sentence.

"Clara just asked me the same thing," Florence said. "Will you two relax? You look like you just saw a ghost."

"Florence, you can't stay here. You know your son won't let you."

"I don't give a damn what Paul says," Florence said vehemently, her hands on her hips, her body shaking like that of a wet dog. "He doesn't own me. I'm too old for him to tell me what to do. I'll do what I want." Then her eyes softened and she began to plead. "Please, Mary, let me stay here with you and Clara. Tell me I can."

"It's just not up to me, Florence," Mary replied. "You know I would love to have you. Come on. Get in here anyway. Come and have a cup of coffee while we put our heads together and try to figure out what we should do."

Clara reached for another mug for Florence. The first one that came to hand said, "Home Is Where the Heart Is." *How appropriate,* she mused. Soon the three sat facing each other. No one spoke. The shock of seeing Florence had yet to wear off. "Well, what was Gretchen's Place like, Florence?" Mary finally asked.

Florence put down her mug. "Well, let me tell you." And she was off and running. When Florence told a story, there was no interrupting her or expecting a brief recap. She was going to tell it all, down to the last detail. "I couldn't imagine where Paul was driving me," she said, settling into her narrative. "It may be in South Port, but it was somewhere I've never seen before, way out on the outskirts of town. Finally, we turned down a side road. I have to admit it was pretty, all shades of green, with spruce and pine trees lining both sides of the long windy drive that leads in to it.

"By the time we arrived, I'd pretty much gotten over being angry with Paul. What was the point? Finally, I saw this sign: 'Gretchen's Place.' A big ol' sprawling colonial revival house, white picket fence—the whole nine yards. Paul drove us right up to the front door. He got out of the car and came around to help me out. I just sat there looking at the place where I was supposed to live for the rest of my life. It was just an ordinary house. What surprised me was that it didn't resemble an institution at all.

"I know Paul was surprised, but he didn't say anything. I'm sure he too was expecting something a bit more formidable. It didn't bother me. I thought it was fine. As we walked in, Paul told me he'd heard wonderful things about it. Apparently, they have a great cook—he knows how much I appreciate a good meal.

"I was immediately startled by two little white barking dogs that came sniffing around my legs. I think they were hoping to pick up a smell of another pooch. Once they were certain I hadn't been in another dog's company, they went trotting off in another direction, on a quest to find something more interesting, I'm sure.

"Just then, a tall, overweight woman of about forty, I'd say, in a long denim dress stepped off the porch to greet us. She had shoulder-length blond hair, pulled back into a ponytail, and she was all business. At the sight of me her lips turned up into the slightest suggestion of a smile. My initial impression was that those lips hadn't gotten much exercise in a long time. I smiled and shook her hand, as did Paul. Her name was Gretchen and she owned the place. We followed her into the house.

"I have to say it was decorated quite nicely. Quality antique furniture," Florence continued. "The walls were painted mustard yellow and Williamsburg blue, befitting the era, which was around the turn of the century. It had beautiful shutters, and colorful colonial curtains at the windows. Hardwood floors shining as if they'd just been polished. You could almost see your reflection in them. The place was spotless. You could tell Gretchen was quite proud of it by the way she emphasized details of the wedding staircase in the front entrance, and the fact that the house was built by a sea captain for his bride."

Florence took a sip of her coffee and continued. "Anyway, where was I? Oh, yes. Gretchen escorted us into the library. I have to tell you, I couldn't help feeling contented, sitting in that room. It was cozy. Gretchen turned out to be quite nice, in spite of her rather authoritarian demeanor. She and Paul talked for what felt like forever about the place. My mind drifted off. I couldn't help thinking about you two. I wondered what you were doing at that very moment. I'd have given anything to be with you instead of the predicament I was about to be thrust into. Pleasant as it was, it wasn't half as nice as your house, Mary."

"Oh, you're just saying that," Mary said modestly.

"Oh, no I'm not," Florence insisted, then continued with her narrative. "Nothing could be as nice as being in the company of you two wonderful people. It didn't seem fair. I had finally found friends I enjoy being with, and Paul had to come and drag me off to a place where I don't know a soul. That's when I started thinking about making my getaway. Before they'd finished talking, I had a complete plan worked out in my mind. I couldn't wait to set it into action.

"So, Gretchen took us on a tour, then finally showed us what was going to be my bedroom. For the

time being, I was down to share a room with Lulu—
and never have you met such a Lulu!

"When I met her, Lulu was lying on her side
with her eyes closed, pretending to be asleep. Our
conversation had no effect on her. She lay curled
up in a fetal position with her blanket pulled up to
her nose. All we could see of her was a head of wild
white hair. Gretchen assured Paul that I would have
the next available private room. She admitted that
Lulu could be, I think her words were, 'difficult' and
'cantankerous' at times. I got the sense that Lulu
could hear every word that was being said, but was
not about to let herself be bothered. She kept her eyes
shut tight the entire time we were all in there.

"Anyway, the room itself was, well, it had its
good points and bad points. It was large and sunny,
but it had pink floral wallpaper that I took an instant
dislike to. My bed was to be the one next to the door,
which would make it easy for what I was planning,"
she said with a conspiratorial wink. Clara and Mary
were following her story with a breathless intensity.

"I went back downstairs, hugged Paul goodbye at
the door, and assured him I'd be fine, then Gretchen
escorted me back to my room and reminded me that
dinner would be served in the dining room at five o'clock
sharp. I got the picture that late was not tolerated.

"As soon as Gretchen left, I started getting ready
to take a little nap when Lulu began screaming for

no apparent reason. I jumped! I walked over to her bedside and put a hand on her shoulder, trying to comfort her. That's when Lulu's hand came up from under the blanket and lashed out at me, just missing my face by inches. Then she began to yell for help! There I was, standing in the middle of the room, frozen. I didn't know what to do. Boy, was I relieved to see a nurses assistant coming to my rescue! One look at me and he knew I'd had my first encounter with the infamous Lulu, he told me afterwards.

"I decided I had to spend the rest of the day somewhere else. I was terrified of what the night would bring, when I'd have no choice but to go back to my room. I decided to sit in the library until dinner. When I got there, I found a woman with a full head of white, tight curls and thin pink glasses sitting in a recliner with her pocketbook in her lap, staring out the window. The room was quiet. She said hello and introduced herself, but I soon forgot her name. Then she opened her purse and placed four pairs of dentures on the table beside her!

"I couldn't believe my eyes. She has a reputation for putting anything that isn't nailed down into her purse, I was told later. It's standard procedure there to keep all valuables tucked neatly out of sight, and especially out of reach. This woman, I was told, could snatch at lightning speed. In the blink of an eye, it would be in her purse. I couldn't help myself. 'What in Sam Hill are you doing with all those dentures?' I asked her. 'Oh, these?' she said. 'I have one for every outfit.'"

Mary and Clara burst out laughing. "No!" Clara gasped. "You're making that up."

"Oh, no, not a word of it," Florence insisted. "So let me tell you about dinner. There I was, seated at this huge, very formal mahogany table, in the company of twelve others. Nobody was talking, except for George and Ed down at the far end of the table. They were trying to outtalk each other about their Navy days, and didn't hear it when a woman asked everyone to bow their heads for a moment of silence. Nor did they hear her when she repeated it. At the third request she screamed, 'Shut up!' at the top of her lungs! It frightened me so much my entire body flinched and I swallowed a mouthful of peas the wrong way and started coughing my head off. George and Ed got the message, anyway. Other than me, the room instantly went quiet. Everyone bowed their heads.

"That's when I realized I had to make my move, and soon," she said in conclusion. Clara and Mary were beside themselves with laughter from her account of Gretchen's Place.

Chapter Forty-Four

Community Rules

Mary knew she had to let Paul know what was going on, but first she called Gretchen's Place. They would be looking for Florence, she knew, and they would be contacting the police, if they hadn't already. She told Gretchen she was a friend of Florence and that she would call Florence's son to let him know Florence was safe and at her house.

"We'll be contacting Mr. Foster, too," Gretchen told Mary. "It's just standard procedure."

Mary sat back down at the table with Florence and Clara. She had to think of how to approach Paul, not just with the news that Florence was with her, but with her appeal for him to reconsider letting Florence stay with them. The kitchen was quiet, as they all sat and pondered the situation.

Mary closed her eyes and prayed about it; Clara was wringing her hands together while Florence wiped a tear from her eyes.

"Your story, and your telling of it, was hilarious. But this is serious business, Florence," Mary finally said. "You can't just walk out of the place without telling anyone and not expect repercussions. Not only are you in trouble, but now you have implicated me as well."

"I'm sorry about getting you involved in this, Mary, but what else could I do?" Florence asked. "I couldn't stay there. It was awful. My roommate kept yelling half the night. A couple of nice nurses' aides tried to give her milk and cookies to try to keep her quiet. I heard her yelling at them to get out and leave her alone. Poor girls. I felt sorry for them. They were just trying to help the old witch. If need be, I'll just go back to my apartment tomorrow."

"Your son won't allow it, Florence, and you know it," Clara said flatly. "Put on your thinking caps, ladies. There has to be a solution to the problem."

After a long silence, Mary spoke. "I think I have it. By goodness, I think I have it!" she said, clapping her hands. The sound snapped Clara and Florence's heads in her direction. "I'll need to make a few phone calls this afternoon but, you know, it really might work."

"What might work?" Clara said. "What are you talking about?"

"Well," Mary said slowly, still thinking out the details as she spoke, "Paul said he wanted Florence to be in a safe environment. I think he's talking about a place like this," she said, pressing both palms together as if in prayer.

Both Clara and Florence stared at her. Then Clara said anxiously, "So ... go on."

"Okay. Think about it, girls. Paul wants Florence in a safe place, a small, homey comfortable place. What I'm going to say to him is this. 'Paul, you put your mother in Gretchen's Place, from what Florence says, it had the look and feel of a home, not an institution. Why not let her stay here, at Mary's Place? It's safe, small, and homey."

Clara cut her off. "Mary," she said, "you're a genius!"

Florence gave her hands one hardy clap and started to laugh. "I love it!" she exclaimed. Mary and Clara joined in laughing, too.

"This could be the start of something wonderful," Mary said excitedly. "I don't know of any law that says I can't have as many friends as I want living here with me. I'm not interested in turning this place into a nursing home. What I envision right now is just the opposite: a place where people simply live together, sharing the same space. Of course, we'll need some rules."

Clara and Florence both nodded in agreement but didn't speak, not wanting to interrupt Mary's train of thought. They could see by the way she was squinting her eyes that more ideas were about to flow through her, like a waterfall gushing from its highest peak. "We'll all need to be responsible for certain chores. For example, I love to cook so I'll take that on."

"I like to clean," Clara said. "You cook, Mary, and I'll clean up the dishes. And you can count on me to keep the place spotless. When I was sick, I let my housework go, but I feel swell now."

"Let's see," Florence said, "what could I do? I know," she said after a moment of thought. "I'll wash and iron clothes. I'm good at that. I'm a good seamstress, too, if anyone needs something mended."

Mary looked from one to the other. "Well, see there? Just look at all the talent in this room. It's important that we stay busy, ladies. My mother used to say idleness is the devil's workshop. Let's not sit around daydreaming and feeling like things are hopeless and out of our control. There's always an answer."

Neither Clara nor Florence could be smiling any wider than they were. "One thing that drives me crazy," Mary went on, "is to hear someone saying they're bored. I've never been bored a day in my life.

There never have been enough hours in a day for me. If the same people that talk about being bored would get off their derrieres and do some volunteering or something interesting and fun, they'd feel better. Is everyone okay with staying busy?"

Both Clara and Florence agreed they wanted to stay busy, and planned to keep going to the day care center. The morning flew by with everyone talking nonstop, trying out ideas for the future on each other. Some they all liked, some earned dubious looks, but they all thoroughly enjoyed the process.

"I just bet my mother is looking down at this moment grinning ear to ear," Mary laughed as they sat in the living room refining their plans. "What could be a better use of this old house than sharing it with others? Goodness knows there's plenty of room. We won't be stepping all over one another."

"There *is* one thing we really should all think about, Mary," Clara said.

"What's that?" she asked, crossing her legs and turning to face Clara, curious about what Clara had on her mind.

"We can't stay here for nothing, Mary. I'd want to pay you for being part of the household. Have you thought about what to charge us?"

"As a matter of fact, ladies, I have," Mary said at her most businesslike. "If I accept money from you, it's like I'm running a business. This is not a business, it's our home. I'm not trying to get rich. Goodness knows, at my age. My house is paid for and, as my aunt Bertha used to say, it don't leak. So, here's what I wanted to ask the two of you. Clara, will you be willing to buy groceries every week?"

Clara nodded in agreement, feeling it was more than generous of Mary. She also knew Mary well enough to know that if she put up a fuss, Mary would win. That's the way it had always been between them.

Florence was equally agreeable to giving Mary enough money to pay all the utility bills. And they all agreed on throwing money into a pot monthly that could be used for maintenance, and anything else they couldn't think of at the moment.

"One last thing," Mary said with a look of seriousness written all over her face. "Like I said, I don't want to ask you to pay rent, not now anyway, but if I ever have to ask you for money, believe me I'll be fair and only ask for what is absolutely necessary."

Just like any new plan, they knew there would be kinks to work out. The main thing was that everyone was in complete agreement as to doing their share. Both Clara and Florence wanted it to work. The alternative—going to live anywhere else— neither wanted to think about. Robert and Darcy were happy Clara was living with Mary. If Mary could convince Paul that Florence living with them would be a good idea, they could put their plan into motion.

Mary called Paul, who answered the phone at the first ring. She was all ready to plead her case. He sounded anxious. "Hi, Paul," she greeted him. "This is Mary. I don't know if the assisted care home has called you or not, but your mother is here."

"I know," he said. "I've had a busy morning. I just got off the phone with Gretchen's Place, and then Robert called me, presumedly at your request. We had a good talk. I appreciated his suggestion to let mother stay with you. I've made up my mind. If you still want her, you have my blessing. I don't mind admitting I was at my wits' end, Mary. My only recourse was to try to get guardianship over mother and *make* her go. Robert couldn't say enough about you. In fact, he has convinced me this is the best thing I could do for her. "You know, Mary, I feel good about all this, and especially that I'm letting Mother do what she wants. 'Whose life is it anyway?' is what I've been saying to myself."

Sitting in the living room by the fire, Florence held her breath the entire time Mary was in the kitchen on the phone with Paul, hoping desperately he'd agree. The last thing she wanted was to fight with him, or even worse, be forced somehow to go back to Gretchen's Place.

Mary returned to the living room, grinning, her arms raised in a V for victory.

"You look like the Cheshire cat," Clara laughed. "Out with it."

"He's agreed!" Mary told Florence jubilantly. "This calls for a celebration!"

Chapter Forty-Five

When I Am Old, I Shall Wear Purple, Take More Chances, and Count my Blessings

A S THE DAYS AND WEEKS rolled by, Mary, Clara and Florence settled nicely into their living arrangement. All of their plans for creating a comfortable community had become a reality. They went about the day enjoying each other's company, and staying busy. Mary was pleased that both Florence and Clara were going to the community center with her. It tickled her that in spite of herself Clara enjoyed chair yoga. Florence, on the other hand, flatly refused to participate. She insisted that the only exercise she was going to get was walking to wherever she needed to go. They all fell naturally into a daily routine, and by the end of the day after dinner and all the chores were done, they retired to the living room to watch the news and enjoy their favorite television programs.

Once everyone had gone off to bed, Mary struggled to keep one eye open as she lounged with her feet up waiting patiently for the ten o'clock news. She decided to make herself a cup of tea. The mug she chose was one of her favorites. It read, "When I Am Old, I Shall Wear More Purple, Take More Chances, and Count My Blessings." She was happier than she ever thought possible.

She put her feet down on the floor and sat up straight, making her seem taller than she was. Her mind was moving from one thought to another like a runaway car without brakes. First, she began thinking about Florence. She was glad Paul was happy about his mother's living arrangement. She'd had several nice conversations with him. He was the kind of son any mother would be proud of. It was clear to Mary that Florence was right in wishing he would find the right person and get married. He'd make a fine husband and father someday.

Darcy was finally finished with that no-account Jeff. She had shared with Mary that she'd had a sick feeling in her stomach ever since she and Stella spoke. She now suspected that he had been lying all along about everything having to do with his marriage. She wondered what else he'd lied to her about. She told Mary she was certain he had no intention of marrying her, and there was no sense fooling herself.

Mary knew Darcy had made the right decision. She knew a smart and pretty girl like her deserved better. She couldn't help thinking someone like Paul, Florence's son, would be a much better choice for her; he was handsome, smart, and nice.

Then Mary's thoughts drifted to Clara. She wished she would invite Dave to come to South Port for a visit. She knew Clara well enough to know she would keep putting off what could be the wisest move she ever made. Dave wanted to see her, and Mary knew that Clara wanted to see him as well. *She's afraid, that's all, plain and simple. But afraid of what?* Mary wondered. *Falling in love at her age?* She, like Clara, had known what genuine love is, the kind of love that has no boundaries, a love that cares not and asks little, a love that is eternal. But Mary's chance at love had come and gone while Clara's chance was about to begin again.

Mary turned off the television and took her cup to the kitchen. She made sure that everything was neat and tidy then headed for bed. She sat on the side of her mattress, head bowed in prayer as she thanked God for her health, her new roommates, and the chance to create a community out of this old house that served everyone.

∞

Meanwhile, Clara lay awake, staring at the ceiling. She couldn't sleep. Darkness had found every nook and cranny of the room. She was overflowing with excitement and overwhelmed with gratitude about how her life was unfolding.

She closed her eyes, wishing sleep would come. She couldn't help thinking about Dave.

Finally, her mind began to quiet, her breathing slowed, she relaxed, and sleep invited itself in. She dreamt of Dave.

Discussion Questions

1. In the beginning of the book, Clara is bothered by strange banging sounds. These sounds are very disturbing to her, and she feels frightened and angry when she cannot locate the source. Her trip to the attic puts a stop to the sounds. Do you think Clara actually hears them, or are they all in her imagination?

2. The dolls and Teddy replace Clara's feelings of loneliness, and they give her a feeling of well-being. Is this a healthy alternative to being around people? Have you ever experienced the "empty nest syndrome"?

3. Have you ever been in a situation where you haven't wanted to do things you previously enjoyed? How did you get out of the rut you were in?

4. When Clara loses her driver's license, it is an extremely traumatic time in her life. Can you identify with her feelings? Are you making plans for what you will do if you lose your driver's license in the future?

5. What advice would you give to people with aging parents who see the need to stop their parents from driving a car or who see the need to take other steps that will result in their parents' loss of independence?

6. In the story, mugs are selected to go along with a mood. Do you find this helps to draw a picture of what the characters are feeling? Can you see yourself doing a similar thing?

7. Clara misunderstands Doctor Hoyt's instructions on how her medications should be taken. What are your feelings about this? Have you ever been confused about how a medication should be taken? Do you think the directions should be in writing and not given over the phone? Do you have a plan in place to make sure you are taking your medication correctly?

8. Mary and Clara's friendship stems from childhood, and their bond is a strong one. Is there someone in your life who means as much to you?

9. What is your opinion of Clara's relationship to her husband, Frank? Do you think therapy

could have helped Clara cope with Frank's depression?

10. Clara's feelings for Dave remained with her throughout her life. How do you feel about her keeping this feeling a secret?

11. Clara's parents made her put the child she had outside of wedlock up for adoption. What are your feelings about how her parents handled the situation? Do you think that the primary factor in her parents' decision was race?

12. Clara's desire to permanently move in with Mary raises very conflicting viewpoints in Robert and Darcy about what is in their mother's best interests. How does this resonate with you? Which opinion would you have had in the situation? Why?

13. Think about yourself aging further. Where do you see yourself living? Can you imagine yourself living in a similar environment as Mary, Clara, and Florence? If not, why?

About the Author

Elizabeth Pettiford is a registered nurse who is dedicated to working with seniors. Her mission is to help create through her novels a positive outlook on aging that inspires people to think out of the box. She sees aging as an important phase in one's life in which life can be lived to its fullest if one is willing to accept change with a positive attitude. She lives in New Hampshire with her husband, Ron.

www.ingramcontent.com/pod-product-compliance
Lightning Source LLC
Chambersburg PA
CBHW071527260626
47170CB00002B/544